A ZHONG FONG
MYSTERY

THE HUA SHAN
HOSPITAL
MURDERS

A ZHONG FONG
MYSTERY

THE HUA SHAN
HOSPITAL
MURDERS

火

DAVID ROTENBERG

McArthur & Company
Toronto

Published in Canada in 2003 by
McArthur & Company
322 King Street West, Suite 402
Toronto, Ontario
M5V 1J2

National Library of Canada Cataloguing in Publication

  Rotenberg, David (David Charles)
  The Hua Shan Hospital Murders / David Rotenberg

  ISBN 1-55278-349-9

  I. Title.

  PS8585.084344H92 2003   C813'.54   C2003-900108-3

Jacket design, f/x / Composition: *Mad Dog Design*
Author photo: *John Reeves*
Printed in Canada by *Transcontinental Printing Inc.*

The publisher would like to acknowledge the financial support of
the Government of Canada through the Book Publishing Industry
Development Program (BPIDP) and the Canada Council for our
publishing activities. The publisher further wishes to acknowledge
the financial support of the Ontario Arts Council and the Government
of Ontario through the Ontario Media Development Corporation's
Ontario Book Initiative for our publishing program.

10 9 8 7 6 5 4 3 2 1

CONTENTS

For Susan, Joey, and Beth

Author's Note

Robert Cowens' family story is based on historical fact.
Some of the names of the characters have been altered
and some of the technical details have been changed to
help the fiction, but the basis of the story is true.

There is no intention in this novel to slander
Manichaean ideals or those who follow this creed.
However, Manichaeism, like all faiths, is subject to
interpretation by its followers. Some of these interpretations
are heinous and turn toward violence. Sometimes this
happens because such interpretations are based on
misreadings of the original texts, or on only partial readings
of those texts, or on readings of deliberately mistranslated
sections of the texts. For whatever reason, the texts are
quoted to support actions that are dangerous to others.
At such times, both those who are of the faith and those
who are not must step forward and be counted. Any
creed that professes to be the only true path must be
questioned. It is in such a light that Manichaeism, and
other faiths, are being held up to scrutiny in this novel.

BEFORE

Fong reached over and touched Lily's cheek. A smile creased her face as, without waking, she tried to kiss his fingers. "Don't get up, Lily," he whispered.

She rolled over and snuggled into his side. "Mine," she sighed.

Fong permitted himself a moment of satisfaction. Their three-month-old daughter Xiao Ming had given them a break. She'd actually slept for five straight hours – a record. Fong pulled back his side of the covers and stood on the ancient wooden floor. He slid his bare feet back and forth along the smoothness of the boards – an old familiar thing.

He looked back at Lily. In sleep her features were so soft. He was grateful for her and Xiao Ming and for the rarest of all things – a second chance.

He entered the bathroom and lit the flame beneath the small rusting water heater connected to the shower. Then he went to see if there was anything to eat. No apartments had kitchens in Shanghai but there was an old breadbox. Inside was a half-eaten pastry that Lily told him was called a palmier. He took a tentative bite then put it back. Wheat-based products were new to him and he didn't care for them. Lily, on the other hand, seemingly couldn't do without them.

He unbuttoned his pyjama top and headed back toward the shower. The glint of light off a polished picture frame on the table drew his eye. So, Lily had finally gotten back the photos and even had one framed.

He lifted the picture and angled it toward the large window that overlooked the courtyard. Laughter burped from his mouth. There he was in a costume from the American Civil War with Lily at his side wearing a very wide green dress with a tight bodice and blond curls – nine-plus months pregnant.

"This itches, Fong," Lily had said as she took a handful of crinoline and yanked it away from her butt.

"Whose fault is that?" said Fong smiling and striking the pose the photographer had shown him.

"Need picture, we do," said Lily changing to English so the photographer couldn't understand what she was saying. Then again even if the photographer spoke English it was doubtful that he could follow Lily's own particular variant of the language. "Proof for *baby that* I married me."

"You sure did, Lily." Fong's English was textbook perfect. It had to be in his position as head of Special Investigations for the Shanghai district.

"Stand still," shouted the exasperated photographer in highly accented Shanghanese.

"What's with the costumes, Lily?" asked Fong in English.

"Very modern, Fong. Do it everybody in Shanghai. Everybody who everybody. Do this. Modern. Hop. Very hop."

"Hop?"

She scowled at him.

"Okay, I think I get that. So who am I supposed to be?"

"Rhett Butler in *Pffftf with the Wind.*"

"*Pffftf with the Wind?*"

"Name of film famous. Famous famous famous."

"Ah that *Pffftf with the Wind.* And who are you supposed to be?"

"Scarlet Hara."

"Ah."

"Ah, yourself."

"Sorry."

"Okay." Lily straightened her wig trying to get two very long blond curls out of her face. In Shanghanese she said, "You look very handsome, Fong."

"And you look quite unusual."

Lily looked at him, not sure what he meant.

"Please," the photographer shouted.

Lily said in English, "Play part Fong. Play part!"

"Please," the photographer pleaded.

"Yeah, Lily, behave yourself."

She made a face and yanked at her crinolines again.

"Still itches?"

"Like mice nibbling my privates."

"Ah."

"More with the ah's from you, husband."

The photographer clapped his hands. "Folks, this is costing you a small fortune. Why not just take the pose, say the line, and I'll shoot you?"

Fong took the pose. "What's the line again, Lily?" he asked under his breath.

"Frankie, my dear I didn't do a dam."

"Really?"

She nodded, stomped her foot and with her best I-love-you-but-I'll-kill-you-if-you-fuck-this-up look said, "Yes, really."

"Who played these roles, anyway?"

"Clark Kent played you. Famous actor, Clark Kent and very good-looking."

"Ah."

"And Vivien Laid play me or Janet Laid – somebody laid played me."

"Ah – I'm sure she did and I'm sure she was."

"What, Fong?"

"Ah, nothing, Lily, " he said putting the prop cigar into his mouth and puffing out his chest as he had been told to do.

"One too many 'ah's' from my leading man, you having way too much fun," said Lily as she stomped down hard on his foot.

Fong howled and chomped down on the cardboard cigar. That was the exact moment captured in the photograph.

Fong laughed out loud, put the picture back on the table, and headed toward the shower.

As he did, a distant roll of thunder echoed across the human vastness that was Shanghai – and Xiao Ming began to cry.

CHAPTER ONE

AN OLD CROSS

Fong looked down at the bones of the half-exposed skeleton that protruded from the slanted side of the Shanghai construction pit – then at the local detective who had called for him. The man was an old-style cop. Almost bald. Definitely tough. Probably right most of the time, but in this case dead wrong. "Officer, I have no idea why you contacted me. It's a skeleton, yes, and at first glance I'd agree that whoever this used to be was a victim of extreme physical trauma . . ."

"You mean he may have been beaten to shit by a fat club or something?"

Fong wouldn't have used those exact words but that was the gist of what he thought. He nodded. A shaft of light pierced through the heavy cloud cover and lit Fong. "Yes officer, this person was probably killed in an assault with a blunt instrument."

"Fuckin' murdered."

Fong liked the man's aggressive gruffness. It made him want to laugh, but in the presence of death, even ancient death, laughter dies quickly. "Yes, that would be my guess officer but I'm with Special Investigations not homicide. I only investigate . . ."

". . . crimes against foreigners, Detective Zhong. I know that." The man spat into the thick mud of the construction pit.

"Then why did you call me?"

"I think the guy – this guy – this dead guy – was wearing this." The cop opened a large, calloused paw. Nestled in the fleshy portions of his hand was a tarnished metal cross on a thin silver chain. Although it was more equilateral than most crucifixes, Fong assumed it was a Christian cross of some sort. Fong took it in his hand. It was surprisingly heavy. Its heft was oddly pleasing. "Was it around his neck?"

"Hard to tell. I found it in the mud behind the neck bones which you might have noticed were crushed."

Fong leaned in closer to the skeleton. No, he hadn't noticed.

The officer held out a Polaroid. It clearly showed the position of the cross stuck in the mud behind the neck bones.

Fong looked up at the officer and raised his shoulders – the pan-China gesture for, "So?"

"You want my guess?"

"I do, officer. Take a guess."

The man picked briefly at his brownish teeth. When he spoke his face revealed nothing, but his voice was a little further forward than before. "Not many Chinese Christians. This was probably some crazy Long Nose who got himself in a bit of trouble."

Fong closed his fingers around the cross. Its weight was suddenly not so comforting.

"How long has the body been here, officer?"

"My forensic guy thinks long. How long? On that he's got no guess."

Fong looked up the wall of the almost completed construction pit that had yielded up the dead man, then back toward the yawning cavity behind him. "What're they building here?"

"Something big. Who knows what?"

Fong nodded. Shanghai was full of empty pits that quickly became big who-knows-whats.

"So I was right Detective Zhong to call you in?"

"Yes. I guess you were, officer."

"Good. Then the case is yours. I'll send you a copy of the initial findings."

"Fine."

The cop began moving up the steep side of the construction pit.

"Where are you going, officer?"

"Home. It's going to rain."

Fong looked up at the sky then down at his hand. The equal-sided cross sat flat on his palm. A fat raindrop spatted right at the crossing of the crucifix's arms. Fong looked up. It wasn't going to rain. No. It was going to pour.

After calling in his forensic team, Fong made his way through the muck of the construction site to the supervisor's hut.

The large man who greeted him there was a classic of his type. A foreman whose only concern was completing the project on schedule, safety be damned – fuck the poor men from the country who lifted and hoisted and toiled in the mud for next to nothing. This kind of man had been put in his place after the liberation but had emerged from his hole to make money in the "New China."

Fong was no card-carrying Communist, but human beings are not animals. They are not meant to be worked from before dawn til after dusk, seven days a week, at labour that might actually kill some of them.

"How long, Mr. Police Man?" barked the foreman.

"As long as it takes," Fong answered – happy to ruin the man's day.

"That's not all that convenient – sir."

"No kidding." Fong enjoyed the shimmer of confusion that crossed the man's face. "Want to make a phone call?"

"To whom?"

"To whoever is the money behind this pit. He'll want to know what's going on here."

"Will he really?"

"They usually do."

"She won't."

"She?"

"As in woman – yes. Madame Faisan's explicit instructions were to finish the work as quickly as possible and avoid the rash of unforeseen difficulties that seem to plague so many large projects in the People's Republic of China."

"And this Madame Faisan lives–"

"Hong Kong now. Kabul before. Apparently the Taliban weren't keen on her."

Fong nodded, only peripherally aware of the Taliban and its doings. A slash of lightning lit the world outside the hut. Then the rain began to pelt down on the corrugated iron roof. The din momentarily deafened both men.

"Well, you can tell Madame Faisan that like the rain, the delay that our investigation will cause is just one of those unforeseen difficulties that do tend to plague business in the People's Republic of China."

"She'll call her political friends and raise hell."

"Raise hell is an interesting phrase," Fong said slowly.

"Why's that?"

Fong didn't bother answering the man. But as he left the hut he mulled over the words: Raise hell. He thought of the skeleton poking up from the ground. Was that raised hell? He permitted himself the indulgence of free association for a moment longer then got back to work.

Fong's forensic team was yellow-taping the area when he returned to the pit. The ground in which the bones had been found was already covered in a thick plastic sheet to keep the rain from further deteriorating the crime site.

The workers were kept back and away as the cops proceeded methodically despite the downpour.

As Fong approached he heard a muffled cry to his left. He turned to see Lily, his wife, mother of their three-month-old baby and head of his forensic team. She was kneeling in the mud, her long black hair pasted by the rain to her lean angular features.

When she saw him, tears welled from her beautiful eyes and mixed with the rain coming down her face. Fong had never seen Lily cry like this before. Then he followed her outstretched hand. There, peaking through the thick mud was the severely weathered skull of a child – no, of a baby.

Despite Lily's pleading look he stepped away from her and forced himself to take in the whole scene.

An adult skeleton on its back, head turned toward the child. The child on its stomach turned away. They were close together.

Close enough to reach out and hold hands.

CHAPTER TWO

DEVIL ROBERT

The rain thrummed against his large umbrella as Robert Cowens stood on the Bund Promenade. A decaffeinated coffee, hard to find in Shanghai, sat cold and unsipped near at hand on the rail. To a casual observer it would seem that Robert was lost in some deep complex thought. But in fact he was trying to recall the lyric to a song.

A gust swept beneath Robert's umbrella and blew his thinning blond hair across his forehead. Robert tasted the salty tang of Yangtze River air and turned to face the Bund building from which the infamous Silas Darfun had controlled an empire.

Robert's usually dancing eyes hardened.

The Chinese men standing in the rain at his side chattered on, seeing none of this. They knew little of the man they referred to as Devil Robert. They did know that Devil Robert was a thing called a Jew, which like everything else in the world as far as they were concerned, had originated in the Middle Kingdom – the remnants of which still existed to this day in Kai Feng. They also understood that, although they didn't like Devil Robert, they needed him to sell the goods they claimed to have plundered from far-off desert airees on the fabled Silk Road.

Robert listened to the Chinese men yatter on, pleased that they were unaware he had learned quite enough Mandarin since his first trip to China four years ago to get the gist of their conversation.

It was prudent to know some Mandarin when a very special part of one's income was made from the illegal buying and selling of Chinese antiquities. True, Robert made the bulk of his money as a lawyer working through an international law firm out of Toronto – but he had never really been satisfied with making large sums of money by making even larger sums of money for people who already had very, very, very large sums of money.

There were more important things in the world than making money – revenge, for example, was more important. But revenge in the People's Republic of China cost money – much more money than it was legal to bring into or move out of the Middle Kingdom.

He looked back at Silas Darfun's building on the Bund, then focused his eyes on a far distant point. His breath settled and a shiver moved through him – he'd remembered the lyric to the song.

He cracked open the tiny memory drawer in his mind and a Joni Mitchell tune slipped out: *I'm travelling in some vehicle; I'm sitting in some café.* And suddenly he was back. Back on the first plane that had brought him to China. The plane was darkened and quiet. People all around him were deep in sleep.

Robert let out a warm breath that misted the window. With his baby finger he printed the words: Silas Darfun rots in hell. As the mist began to fade, taking the writing with it, another message on another frosted window came back to him. His mother's angry scratch in the cold frost of his bedroom window when he was nine years old. It was just one word – and misspelled at that: BECAUS! It was the last thing his crazy mother did before she doused herself in gasoline and set herself alight in front of Robert and his two brothers – *No, Mommy! No Mommy no!*

It was the final mad act of her mad life. It scared Robert in many ways. Not the least was an intense, debilitating fear of fire – of any sort.

Robert looked back at the airplane windowpane. Only one word remained, fading quickly in the mist: Hell.

"Hell – Becaus – what's the difference," he thought.

He put the new CD he'd bought at the airport into his player and punched play.

"I'm travelling in some vehicle,
I'm sitting in some café."

Joni sang in his ear. He reached for the CD jacket and read the title of the piece: "Hejira" – the journey. He pressed replay.

"I'm travelling in some vehicle,
I'm sitting in some café."

"Some vehicle, some café, with you on that, Joni," he thought. She'd always been like a guide. Even as a teenager she'd shown him the way. But he was careful where she led. Loneliness was a seductive but dangerous atoll.

Robert didn't sleep on the plane or watch the endless movies that first flight to Hong Kong. He used the sixteen hours to consider what he wanted to do with what was left of his life. He discarded the immediate response – to find a new lover – and decided that he needed a new direction. A real purpose. Then he thought of his father's words about Silas Darfun and knew beyond any doubt what that real purpose had to be.

In Hong Kong he'd been met at the airport by a lot of flash and glitter. But he was used to that as the point man in the law firm's film deals in Hollywood and Europe. Then a silk-clad woman in her late thirties hopped into the back of the limo and sat beside him. Her exquisite features were set off by delicate makeup that highlighted her cheekbones and her amazing eyes. "If this is a Hong Kong hooker, this is not good," he thought. Then she spoke. She was no hooker – it was worse. She was a producer.

He played an old game he'd perfected in law school. He watched her beautiful lips move as they formed the words but he totally ignored the sounds themselves. It allowed him to appear to be listening but not take in a single word. At the hotel he hopped out and slammed the door behind him before she could follow him. She was just a producer but he was the lawyer – he represented the money. "In this game, sweetie, my one-eyed Johnny beats your three tens."

The days in Hong Kong had been predictable in content if not style. The movie business was basically practised the same all over the world. But as he was packing up to leave, the lady producer from the first day arrived unannounced at his hotel room door.

She was no longer wearing silk. Now she was all business – black suit, black sheer hose, black pumps with just a little more heel than usual. She carried an unfashionably large briefcase.

"Your dealings were fruitful, I hope," she said and flashed him a smile.

He nodded.

"Good. You see the potential benefits in doing business in the Middle Kingdom?"

He nodded again.

"Good. My people . . ."

"Your people?" Robert stopped her.

"My people in Shanghai – those for whom I speak . . . would like you to represent their interests in further projects."

Robert didn't nod this time. He just canted his head a little to one side and waited.

She walked into the bedroom, put the briefcase on the bed, and snapped open the latches. Robert stepped forward to get a peek at the contents, but she angled it away from him. Then she smiled. "My associates and I are prepared to reward you handsomely for representing our interests." Before he could respond she added, "I see you are listening to my words this time, not just watching my lips move, Mr. Cowens. I went to law school, too." She turned the briefcase toward Robert.

Until that very moment Robert had never seen a Buddhist temple scroll. He assumed they were valuable. He also assumed that they were not strictly legal to export.

"And these would be?" he prompted.

"From the Taklamakan Desert. Antiquities worth a fortune to collectors in the West."

Robert forced a smile to his face. "And how would these things get to the West?"

She met his smile with one that was far warmer and inviting than his own. "I would do that for you . . . this time. All you do is find us the appropriate discreet lawyers that such transactions would need. After, I meet you in New York and show you how good 'good' can get." She moved her lips but made no sounds.

Here was the possibility of an insulated source of cash – the special income – he'd need if he really wanted to unearth the secrets of one Silas Darfun. This insulated income could get him around the currency restrictions both coming and going from the People's Republic of China. Yes, this 'antiquing' – as he thought of it – was just the kind of business he'd need. As the card players in his father's club would have called it – a real cash business.

"So?" she asked.

"When do I start?"

That had been four years ago. And finally after earning tens of thousands of dollars "antiquing," and spending every cent of it on bribes, he felt he was closing in on Silas Darfun and his revenge.

The thud of the rain on his umbrella brought him back to the present.

Robert stretched, pulling the long tails of his shirt out of his pants. He sighed – shirts used to stay in his pants. Now they popped out when he stretched. Forty-four years will do that.

He turned to his Shanghanese translator, a round-faced pixie of a woman with bad teeth, a charming smile, and impeccable English. She stood perfectly still, and entirely dry, beneath a small black parasol.

"Mr. Cowens?" she asked.

Not for the first time Robert was pleased that she was plain-looking. His weakness for attractive Asian women had ended his first marriage and derailed any plans for a second. But unlike Silas Darfun, Robert never married his Asian mistresses – and, of course, he had no children with them – or anyone else.

"Mr. Cowens?"

He held a finger to his lips. She bowed her head slightly and waited. A smile crossed his face. His eyes twinkled. "Tell these gentlemen that their product is as phony as a drag queen's tits." He always liked the way she translated profanity. She thought for a moment then asked politely if drag queens were men wearing woman's clothing. He said yes. Then she asked if they were actors like in the Peking Opera. He said, "No, not like that." She nodded that she understood then turned to the Chinese men.

"So what did fuck-face say?" demanded the leader.

"Mr. Cowens suggests that the manuscript you are trying to sell him is less than fully authentic. In fact he stated that it is as fake as a man with succulent mammary glands."

Robert smiled – "succulent" hadn't been part of what he had said. That tidbit said something about his translator – about her sexual orientation, perhaps. That, in turn, answered a lot of questions about her, the way the Chinese treated her – with a stiff, angry indifference, the way she stayed aloof, her acceptance of the ostracism inherent in working for foreigners.

He smiled again. He liked questions to be answered.

Naturally the Chinese men began vociferously defending the authenticity of their offering. Robert picked up a few of the phrases – "directly from Khotan," "the best find in years from the Taklamakan," "he's being a long-nosed idiot," "we're insulted by the accusation," and so on and so on – blah, blah, blah. Robert wondered what the Mandarin word for blah was, then set it aside – who cared?

Robert took the plastic-wrapped scroll they were trying to sell him from his briefcase and held it out to them. Sir Auriel Stein had unmasked this kind of forgery more than a hundred years ago, right at the beginning of the mad rush by Europeans to rape the Silk Road's desert temples of their sacred texts, statuary, and frescos.

The men protested loudly but didn't bother reaching for the scroll. That sealed it. If the scroll were even remotely valuable they would have snatched it back from him. But they didn't. They just made noise.

"Enough." His voice cut through the babble of complaint. The men stopped and stared at him. Chinese were loud-spoken by nature but were always surprised when a Westerner raised his voice. Robert chuckled to himself. Just an old trick – raising the voice – but a good one. He put out his hand and whispered to his translator, "Don't translate this." He bowed slightly to the men, tilting water from his umbrella as he did so, put the fake scroll back in his briefcase – never know when a fake could come in handy – and smiling, yet again, said, "Fuck you very much." Then he added, "See you a year from Simchas Torah." He looked at his translator and inquired, "Don't know how to translate that, do you?"

She smiled back and said, "No, Mr. Cowens, I don't."

"Good," he said, "how 'bout lunch before we meet the next set of charlatans?" She nodded, dismissed the Chinese men, and led the way, unaware that Robert momentarily lingered – his eyes glued to the window high up the Bund building from which Silas Darfun had ruled an empire and perhaps ruined Robert's life.

Forked lightning snapped into being above the building. Robert smiled and said under his breath, "Devil Robert's closing in on you, you old fuck."

CHAPTER THREE

AT HOME

Lily stood by their rain-streaked apartment window that overlooked the courtyard on the grounds of the Shanghai Theatre Academy. Xiao Ming was lying on a blanket to one side. Usually at this hour the baby was with Lily's mother, but because it was the first Monday of the month the old woman had to attend her building's party meeting.

Fong stood across the room from Lily, waiting.

"I'm sorry, Fong."

"Don't be, Lily."

"It just – I just put my hand into the mud and – it surprised me."

Fong looked at his strong-willed wife and wondered at the change in her since she'd given birth to Xiao Ming.

"I understand, Lily. I really do," he said opening his arms to her. She moved toward him and allowed him to pull her close. She snuggled into the hard body of her middle-aged husband knowing that he really didn't understand.

He held her to him knowing that she knew that he didn't really understand.

She pecked him on the cheek, handed him a photograph, and returned to the window. Then she turned and addressed him like a dim-witted student, "Think time, Fong," she announced in her personal variant of the English language. She indicated the photograph in his hand and the empty vertical space to the left of the window and said, "It beautiful fits here, Fong."

For an instant Fong recalled a similar translation error on a sign in a major Nanjing Lu department store. The small plaque outside the lady's dressing rooms had said in English, "Women have fits here." He smiled, then looked away.

"Nothing's funny here, Fong," Lily snapped reverting to her beautiful Shanghanese. "It's a rare find. Totally unique." Then to add a practical justification she added, "And just the right size." Fong didn't care about the latter. But Lily was right. The central figure of the stone piece was exquisite.

"No!" Fong said too loudly, then put the photograph back on top of the others on the table.

Lily folded her arms across her chest. "Why?"

"Because I'd be uncomfortable with it, Lily," said Fong, anxious not to know why he was resisting.

"But why, Fong? Give me a reason," Lily demanded.

Before he could reply, Xiao Ming began to cry. The baby seemed to sense even the slightest tension between her parents. The smallest disagreement was met with angry wails of protest. It confused Fong.

Lily reached down and picked up Xiao Ming. Fong stared at the image of his wife and baby. Lily was never so beautiful as when she pulled aside her blouse and, releasing a breast, suckled their daughter. Beautiful, but somehow distant – somehow complete without him. That confused him too.

As the child sucked happily – her tiny, slender fingers and soft palms cupping her mother's breast – Fong picked up the photograph of the ancient fresco. The single standing male with his arms up, palms toward the heavens, dominated the piece. The man's features were partially obscured but clearly they were not Han Chinese.

"Where did you get it, Lily?"

"Think of it as a riddle, Fong."

"What?"

"A riddle. Figure it out."

"You're the one who's good at riddles Lily, not me."

"True. Have you heard this one, Fong? No one at my lab could solve it."

"Lily . . ." This too confused him. When had his wife become enamoured of riddles? What was next – jokes?

"Okay. Listen carefully, Fong. Ready?" Fong nodded. "Good. Okay. Here it is. A man and his son are in a terrible car accident. The father is instantly killed and the boy is badly hurt. He is rushed to the hospital and right into the operating room. The surgeon comes running in, takes one look at the boy and screams: My son! Now, Fong, how can the surgeon be the boy's father when the boy's father died in the car crash?"

"That's it?"

"Yes."

"That's the riddle?"

"Yes."

"Not much of a riddle, Lily. Obviously the surgeon is not the boy's father – the surgeon is the boy's mother."

Lily looked at him, disappointed.

"Is that right, Lily?"

"Yes."

"Good. Now answer my little riddle. Where did you get the photographs of the frescos?"

The baby released Lily's nipple, looked at her father, then rolled back to her previous position. Lily grimaced as the baby bit down hard.

Lily looked at Fong. Her husband. Father to their baby. Her boss at Special Investigations. "I got them in the market."

"From a Tibetan?'

"In fact, she was a Tibetan. A very cute Tibetan, Fong. I think you would have found her attractive."

"Lily-"

"Fong, everything here belonged to you and Fu Tsong. Even this apartment was hers. It's in the Shanghai Theatre Academy because she was an actress here. I am not an actress, Fong. What am I doing here?" She threw up her arms and let out a sigh. "If we are going to stay here I need things that are mine — that belong to me — not her. That," she said, pointing at the ancient fresco in the photograph, "will belong to me and I need it."

Fong glanced out the window. It had stopped raining. Brilliant sunshine bathed the courtyard. A young inebriated student actor staggered across the courtyard singing loudly. Fong didn't want to admit that he was past the point in his life of making a new home. Of shopping and selecting and caring for things. He was actually anxious to rid himself of possessions, and here his young wife was desperate to start collecting.

He didn't know what to say.

The baby let go of Lily's nipple with a slight plopping sound, then let out a loud fart. The sweet smell of baby poop filled the room.

That confused Fong as well.

"I've got to get back to the office," Fong said.

"My mother'll be back in half an hour. I'll see you in forensics in about an hour."

"Sure."

He didn't move to kiss her goodbye. He just stared at her and Xiao Ming - so complete - in and of themselves.

CHAPTER FOUR

ANGEL MICHAEL AND SKELETONS

Angel Michael kept his eyes tightly shut through the last jagged edges of the pain. He waited until the tide of hurt ebbed far from the shore, then he opened his eyes. He was sitting alone, head bowed, in a brilliant pool of post-storm sunlight that streamed through the window of his room on the sixty-fifth floor of the Shanghai Metron Hotel. He turned to the light and watched it separate into its colours as it passed through a tiny imperfection in the glass pane. Putting out his hand, he allowed the rainbow to colour his skin. "This is the light revealed," he said, then looked down at the coffee table in front of him. He carefully cracked the thin glass of the last of the old-fashioned flash bulbs from the pack. Then he sprinkled the phosphorus onto the polished surface. He looked at the chemical strands and said to the empty room, "Threads of light."

He carefully swept the phosphorus into a Ziploc bag, then shallowed his breathing like a monk does before a full night of prayer. But the man in the light was not praying. No. Angel Michael was not praying. He was bathing in the light and planning how to release the light inside himself – the light he had first experienced when he was a six-year-old boy in a small Virginia town, in the farm country outside of Washington, DC.

Shanghai's new police commissioner opened his office window allowing the rain-scoured air to refresh the large room. He wore his party status lightly this day – like he wore his Western-style suits. Fong had heard he was better educated than his predecessors. It was rumoured that he even read a little English. But he was still a party man – a politico. Fong knew that to be named the police commissioner of Shanghai his party loyalty would have been severely tested and found unwavering.

"All I'm asking is an explanation, Zhong Fong," the commissioner repeated as he returned to his seat behind his overlarge desk. There was a knock at his door. "Come," he called without taking his eyes from Fong.

The new head of CSU entered with two of his officers. The commissioner nodded at them. They nodded back – all very chummy. It was obvious they knew what this meeting was about and were preparing to enjoy Fong's discomfort.

"Sir," Fong said, "I understand the chain of command at Special Investigations–" Shit, I had a lot to do with setting it up in my first stint as head of Special Investigations, he thought but decided not to add out loud.

The commissioner made noises meant to placate him then returned to his theme, "Why are you pursuing the investigation into the skeleton in the construction pit?"

"It could fall within Special Investigations' mandate, sir." Fong didn't bother adding that winter was fast approaching and the foreign population in the city was falling off dramatically, which made things slow in his office since all their cases had to involve foreigners. But the commissioner knew that. So why was he making such a big deal about this? Then he sensed another kind of antagonism in the office.

Something personal.

Fong looked at the four men and put it together quickly. They were all younger than him. It was very possible – not likely, but possible – that his return from west of the Wall had scuttled their plans for advancement. Tough, he thought. Then he revised that. The deal he'd struck in far-off Lake Ching had given him back his job. It was a fair deal from Fong's point of view. But from the point of view of these men, Fong's actions could well seem like those of a connected man – a party hack. From their perspective Fong had acted very much like an old-style party member – something Fong had fought against his whole life. It made him very uncomfortable, but he wasn't about to give up his position to appease these men – no matter what they thought.

He was head of Special Investigations and he'd follow up any damn case he wanted. Besides, Fong, although he would adamantly deny that he was superstitious, was a true believer when it came to intuition. And his intuition was screaming at him that there was something important in this case – although for the life of him he couldn't even venture a guess as to what that could be.

"Anything else?" Fong asked.

"As a matter of fact there is – this," said the commissioner as he tossed a departmental form on the desk. His smile was unpleasant.

Fong glanced at the document. "Oh shit," he thought.

The commissioner's smile widened. "It seems you flunked your firing range test . . . again, Detective Zhong."

Fong picked up the form. He was a lousy shot. He'd always been a lousy shot. "I'll retake the test," he said and paused just a breath then added, "Sir." Before the commissioner could answer, Fong took his leave muttering, "I'll be with the skeleton."

* * *

Robert Cowens fingered the sixth 1,000-yuan note, then put it by the eel merchant's right hand. The man continued slicing the freshwater delicacy with his razor blade and laying the long thin strips side by side on his cutting board. He nodded toward a brown package at his feet. Robert picked it up, handed it to his translator, and they headed deeper into the vast street market. Once they were safely away from the eel merchant, Robert's translator opened the package. As they made their way through the thick crowd she whispered her translation of the government file just loudly enough for Robert to hear.

Robert walked and listened trying to envision the Japanese-occupied Shanghai of January 1942. The attack on Pearl Harbor had only been a month earlier and already the German High Consul had arrived with the "final solution" for Shanghai's latest European guests.

The picture the document painted was not new to Robert although some of the details brought new issues to life. But as the translator droned on and on, the voice that came into Robert's ears was that of his youngest brother: "No, Mommy. No Mommy no." And the smell of fire that was quickly followed by a wave of fear so intense that Robert almost fainted.

* * *

"It was what?" Fong shouted.

Lily gave him a don't-use-that-tone-of-voice-with-me look. They were in the forensics lab – her domain since the old coroner had died at her side on a plane to Beijing some twenty months ago. She softened her features and snarked in English, "Too much small head for you understand?"

The two street cops at Fong's side gave each other a quick look and busied themselves with their notepads. The subject of Fong's return with Lily from west of the Wall, his reinstatement as head of Special Investigations, his marriage to Lily culminating in the birth of a baby girl some three months ago made for rich veins of gossip throughout the station. But everyone was careful to keep their thoughts to themselves. Fong was their boss, and Lily's temper was the stuff of legend. And, oh yes, both were extremely good at their jobs.

"Let's speak in the Common Tongue – the boys are getting antsy."

"Fine," Lily replied in her beautiful lilting Shanghanese. "Fine, perhaps your small mind is incapable of understanding the facts forensic science clearly has placed before you."

"That may well be. So try me in simpler terms."

Lily let out a breath, more a sigh of resignation – something deeply Chinese. The two cops waited. She turned back to the autopsy table. The skull, neck bones, clavicle, upper arm bones, part of the rib cage, and one full set of digits were arranged on the metallic surface.

"What happened to the rest?" Fong asked.

"Animals maybe. More likely carried away by the construction crew before they spotted what they'd disturbed in the ground."

"And the facts that forensic science so clearly puts in front of us – one more time please, Lily."

"Male. Caucasian. Mid-life like someone else in the room although he'd be somewhat older now."

"You're losing me again."

"Well, Fong, if he were alive today I'd say he'd be close to 350 years old – give or take a decade or two."

"Are you saying this Long Nose's been dead for almost four hundred years?"

"Give or take ten – maybe twenty."

The cops put down their pads. One mumbled, "Is this for real?"

"We can't catch guys who committed crimes last week, why are we concerned with stuff like this?" blurted out the other cop.

"Because . . ." all eyes swivelled to Lily, ". . . of this." She held up the even-sided crucifix. "And this." She lifted the top-side of the two sets of neck bones and placed the cross, face side down, against the bottom set. After a little prodding it sat in place. Then she put the front set of neck bones on top of the crucifix. The bones fitted perfectly around the metal thing.

She looked at Fong.

"A crucifix bone sandwich. I'm sure the new McDonald's by Renmin Park will have it on the menu by next week," said Fong.

"Only if we tell them about it, Fong," said Lily. With a wicked smile she added, "No more Dim Sum killer stuff, huh."

The men snickered. Fong gave them a look then without raising his voice said, "If it gets out, you're both on garbage detail for a year. Someone has to make sure Shanghai's recycling effort is successful."

In English Lily said, "You done big bad boss being?"

Fong replied, "Sure."

Lily smiled. In Shanghanese she said, "Besides, Fong, the cross sort of stuck in his throat. That could be bad for business."

"No kidding." He shifted his position and a darkness crossed his delicate features. "So cause of death was a crushed throat, right?"

"We can't be sure without more of the skeletal bones, but the damage to these throat bones would be enough to cause death, assuming he wasn't already dead."

"He wasn't," Fong said. "The chin's not broken on the skull is it, Lily?"

"No, Fong, it's fully intact."

The darkness on Fong's face intensified as he said to Lily in English, "He was still alive."

"How do . . ."

Fong turned to the taller cop and said, "Lie down."

The man looked for an explanation but when it quickly became clear that Fong had no intention of explaining his order the man simply lay down on his back.

Fong crossed to the man's right side and raised his foot

quickly then snapped it downward, stopping less than an inch above the man's fully exposed throat.

The man's eyes went large – no, huge – and he involuntarily moved his chin up to avoid the foot hitting his face.

"It's a reflex," said Fong. "We protect our faces even when it exposes other more vulnerable parts. Only live people have reflex actions, Lily."

She nodded.

Fong removed his foot and the cop rolled to one side.

"So those neck bones were crushed when the man was still alive. Which leads to one other question."

"And that would be, Fong?"

Fong went over to the skeleton and removed the top layer of damaged neck bones exposing the equal-sided cross. Fong counted the neck bones down to the top of the cross then turned to Lily and counted the same number down her throat with his finger. His finger came to rest well below her larynx.

Lily repeated her question, "And what one other question would that be, Fong?" ignoring the position of Fong's finger on her neck.

Fong dangled the crucifix on its chain and said in a hoarse voice, "How did they terrify this guy so thoroughly that he agreed to swallow this?"

A thick silence filled the room. Fong allowed the cross to dangle from his fingers. Finally he turned to the cops, "Find me someone who knows about things like this." The light bounded off the crucifix and momentarily flickered across Lily's face. There was fear in her beautiful eyes. The image of a man on his knees, his mouth pried open and the metal thing shoved down his throat – no matter how far in the past – was a thing of childhood nightmares.

Fong indicated to the two cops that they should leave. Once they were gone he turned to Lily, "So?"

Lily opened a side drawer and took out a small object

wrapped in a white linen cloth. She put it on the table and pulled aside the cloth.

The tiny skull looked paper thin and ready to crumble.

Lily let out a long line of sweet breath then said, "It's from the same time as the adult skeleton – perhaps the exact same time."

Fong waited, knowing there was more to come. Finally Lily spoke, "A quick DNA scan suggests there was a relationship between the adult and the child." A bitterness, sour, from dark places entered her voice as she added, "They murdered the baby with the father."

"So it would seem," Fong replied, but he wasn't sure that Lily was right about what happened all those years ago. It was finding the cross and the baby together that had his attention. Could this have been some bizarre religious murder? Such things were unheard of in secular China, but there were always rumblings – troubling rumblings.

"Fong, please . . ." Lily began in a voice that cried out for Fong to comfort her. But he didn't. And he didn't know why he didn't.

Angel Michael's state-of-the-art laptop was blinking when he returned from his late afternoon travels. He shucked off the coat that hid his worker's overalls and punched two function keys. The website www.uofs.w.alberta.ca came up slowly. Along the left side were highlighted icons – class schedules, campus maps, professor's bios, etc. The page itself had some basic palaver about the university – the usual totally inept academic advertising. Normal. Nothing to attract attention. Nothing out of the ordinary. Very common in every respect except one – there is no such university.

Angel Michael quickly scrolled down to Courses and clicked on Political Science. Slowly a new list appeared from top to bottom. He scrolled down to a fourth-year course with the terse title: Justice. He clicked on the underlined word.

A small box appeared at the bottom of the page. There were no instructions in the box.

Angel Michael moved his cursor to the left of the small box and clicked once. Then to the right of the box and clicked again. Then above and below. Upon the last click the cursor within the box began to blink.

Angel Michael typed in his password – FROM THE MOUTHS – and hit enter. The screen went blank then a large black cross filled the space. Eight pop-up boxes snapped on. This was no low-speed peripheral site.

A counter at the bottom flashed the number 6.

"So they wanted to talk again, did they?" thought Angel Michael as the blood vessel behind his eye began to pulse.

He right-clicked on the number and punched in his second password: BY THE LIGHT.

There was a pause, then in the chat box appeared the words: "Welcome Michael."

"Hi," he typed.

"Is Angel Michael's flaming sword in hand?"

"Not yet," he lied. The pain swelled.

"When?"

"When I think it's safe," he lied again.

Just for the slightest moment the chat box was empty – as if the person on the other end was holding his breath. Finally text appeared. "God be with you." The first wave of pain crashed behind his left eye.

Angel Michael turned off the computer without exiting the program and sat in the growing darkness trying to will away the pain. "Before the light – darkness," he quoted. The idea comforted him. He crossed to the window and took out five stick matches from his pocket. He scraped them against the glass. They screeched like fingernails on a black board then flared light . . . and the pain started to recede.

He looked out at the vastness that was Shanghai. He was

alone in this strangest of strange cities. Just the way he wanted it.

And despite what he had said in the chat room, his first message was already in place and ticking its way toward zero – toward the future rising of the light.

CHAPTER FIVE

THE IAGO CONUNDRUM

"This is not a play about a dumb nigger!" shouted the towering Afro-American actor playing Othello as he lifted the middle-aged English actor playing Iago by the throat and held him against the stage-left proscenium arch.

"The Iago Conundrum," said Fong under his breath from his seat at the back of the Shanghai Theatre Academy's decrepit old theatre. It had been his wife's, Fu Tsong's, favourite performance space and she had performed all over China and Japan.

The Caucasian playing Iago was unable to speak. "Good," Fong thought, "every bad actor silenced was a move in the right direction."

"You do that 'I'm-a-bad-dude' shit one more time Gummer and I'll take your stupid British head off your wimpy British body – got it!"

Gummer nodded and the massive black American released his single-handed grip. "Good," he muttered and stomped away.

As soon as he was gone, Gummer turned to the auditorium, and shielding his eyes from the lights, shouted, "Roger, I was only doing what you directed me to do – wasn't I?"

The Iago Conundrum, Fu Tsong, Fong's deceased wife, had called it. It was a classic stage-acting problem. Shakespeare insists that Iago dupe Othello over a remarkably short period of time into murdering his own wife – and all on stage. The audience must know what Iago is doing to follow the plot but at the same time Othello must not. If Iago plays his part so that the audience can follow every twist and turn of his scheming then Othello is made to look like a fool – or as the Afro-American actor so charmingly put it – a dumb nigger. However, if Iago plays his cards too close to the chest, thus making his words totally believable to Othello, it is very possible that the audience will miss the joy of following the scheming – point by point. The Iago Conundrum.

The director wisely sidestepped Mr. Gummer's question and called for a scene without his two male leads. The actresses playing Othello's wife, Desdemona, and Iago's wife, Emilia, were sent for.

Fong looked around the theatre. Its mustiness was familiar. Comforting. He'd spent many, many joyous hours here watching his brilliant wife rehearse and perform. Since her death, he'd haunted the theatre – finding it a good place to think. There was hubbub and chaotic energy everywhere, but since none of it concerned him directly he found a profound stillness amidst the whirlwind. A deep peace to which he often retreated. Lily didn't know. She wouldn't have approved. He didn't want to have to explain.

He fingered his copy of *Othello*. Fu Tsong had played Desdemona. She had used the very script that sat in his lap with its Mandarin on the left and its English translation on the facing page. On some pages she had written notes about the text – insights etched in her remarkably delicate hand. He treasured them as access points to her. To her privacy.

She'd loved Shakespeare's plays and had made Fong read and discuss them with her as she developed her characters. It was during one of these discussions that she'd told him of the Iago conundrum. Like so many memorable conversations with

Fu Tsong it'd taken place mid-coital. He was on his back, she straddling his legs.

"Inside hug," she'd announced as she tightened her muscles around his member – and he'd gasped. Then he opened his eyes and saw her staring down at him.

"What?" he'd protested.

"You like it when I take control," she said sliding her right foot forward so she could push off and rise up and down his length. "You like that."

"So?" he'd croaked.

"So why do you resist me?" she'd asked and quickly rose and fell twice. "Don't you want to be swept away, to be bowled over, to fall hopelessly in love?"

He nodded slowly.

"Then why do you resist? Give over!"

Fong slipped a foot over her bent knee and dragged himself to a sitting position. They were equal now. He rose when she did and fell as she fell.

She smiled.

"What?" he demanded again.

"In your head this feels better – less being swept away – but Fong, in your heart this feels like you've stopped a mighty river. And of course in your thing you feel nothing." Then she'd smiled broadly and announced, "It's the Iago Conundrum of Sex."

"What?" he'd asked yet again.

"You have to work on your vocabulary husband – how many 'what's' is that in one sex session?" Then she'd explained the conundrum. At the end she said, "However, in the Iago Conundrum of Sex there's a way out."

"How? I'm not backing down, Fu Tsong," he announced through gritted teeth as he followed each of her rises and falls so that no one led and no one followed. Nor did anyone get much pleasure.

"How?"

Fu Tsong said, "Like this." She tightened her muscles again and announced, "Inside hug." He gasped and stopped his resistance. "A little something I'm sure Desdemona would know all about. Now Fong, let go. Have the faith that I will bring you safely home. Have a little faith, husband."

As the image of Fu Tsong's memorable inside hug faded, the actress playing Desdemona in this production stepped onstage. Fong's jaw almost hit his chest.

Fong had never seen the famous Chinese film actress Tuan Li in the flesh. Although lovely in film, she was luminous in person.

At the far side of the theatre, Robert Cowens watched Tuan Li steal every eye. He had finally completed a particularly complicated bit of "antiquing" and was anxious to take his mind off what he had just learned about Shanghai in the early forties. And what better way to forget than to be with Tuan Li? For an instant he thought that despite her beauty she wasn't worth all the trouble she'd caused him. Then he dismissed the thought as bullshit. Robert was many things – but a bullshitter was not one of them.

Tuan Li was well aware of her effect on both the men and women in the room. She was also deeply honoured to play the part of Desdemona in the same theatre where the great Fu Tsong had made the role famous. She allowed her eyes to scan the seats. Could the small, delicate-boned man at the back be Fu Tsong's husband? It was rumoured that he was here on occasion.

Then her eye caught Robert and she smiled. Not at him – but definitely for him.

CHAPTER SIX

A BOMB AND A BABY CARRIAGE

The next morning, Lily's elderly mother picked up Xiao Ming as she usually did just before 7 a.m. "Where to today, Mom?"

"The Children's Palace."

Lily had walked past the former mansion almost every day of her married life on her way to work. She'd avoided going into it because it was a place for "artistically inclined children." No doubt Fong's first wife, Fu Tsong the actress, would have spent time as a child in such a place.

"I like to watch."

"Watch what, Mom?"

"Foreigners. They love to see our children and they also come to see the house, which I think was built by some famous foreigner."

"Could be." Lily bent down, kissed Xiao Ming, then touched her mother's fingers lightly. Mother and daughter were much closer now that Lily had a baby.

Before 8 a.m. Lily walked quickly past the long line of women waiting for therapeutic abortions in the Hua Shan Hospital. Although Lily had been sexually active since she was eighteen, she'd always been very careful about birth control and never had to avail herself of China's free answer to overpopulation. And now that she and Fong had their child she had re-instituted her strict birth control regimen of spermicide in addition to the IUD she'd had implanted shortly after Xiao Ming's birth.

But these sad-eyed women at the clinic, many from the countryside, faced the stern governmental consequences of having more than one child and waited stoically to be "unpregnanted."

"At least only a few were showing," Lily thought as she hustled by them. She ascended the long set of steps to her office that was situated directly above the Hua Shan's six operating theatres, which performed more therapeutic abortions in half a week than were done in a month in most American hospitals.

Twenty-three minutes after Lily entered her lab, a therapeutic abortion operating theatre in the People's Twenty-Second Hospital down by the Huangpo River burst into flames.

Seven people were instantly immolated – one doctor, three nurses, two technicians, and of course, poor Ms. Wu who was on the table. By some people's count there were not seven human lives lost in the blast but rather eight – assuming Ms. Wu wasn't carrying twins.

It certainly was the way that Angel Michael and his people counted.

But it wasn't the blast that brought frantic calls to Special Investigations – it was the scrawled note found at the hospital's reception desk moments before the blast – the note was in English. It said: THIS BLASPHEMY MUST STOP.

Fong carefully sealed the note in a plastic evidence bag. All around him sirens were screaming and people were staring bug-eyed, some through dust-encrusted faces.

Fong recognized the growing possibility of real panic taking hold and in a city the size of Shanghai – eighteen million at night, twenty-four million during the day – panic was not an acceptable response to any situation. Fong immediately called in every available man and began issuing orders. "Evacuate the hospital. Cordon off six full square blocks. Anyone acting erratically is to be removed from the area immediately. Block and building wardens are instructed to use whatever force is necessary to keep people indoors."

Fong ordered the yellow-taping of the entire front lobby and then left four young cops on guard with the strict orders that, "Nothing – but nothing – is to be touched. Get the basics from the man at reception who found the note, then bring him down to my office." The police officers nodded and Fong headed toward the blast site. He wanted to talk to Wu Fan-zi.

Fong passed by the security cordon and stepped through the blasted-out wall of the surgery. The place still radiated heat in sporadic pulses. The remains of the foam poured on it by the People's Third Fire Brigade were still very much in evidence. The room was now a shattered twisted thing. Everything pushed upward or outward. Metal shards of expensive machinery thrust deep into the walls and ceiling, glass everywhere, blood, identifiable fragments of human body parts – and amidst the chaos a perfectly formed tiny human fetus wrapped in some kind of metal sheathing inside a metal cage. On the metal sheathing was etched a repeat of the warning – in English: THIS BLASPHEMY MUST STOP.

"What does it say, Fong?"

Fong looked up into the dark, patient eyes of Wu Fan-zi, his head arson investigator – his fireman. Fong searched for a good translation for the word *blasphemy* in Mandarin. He finally settled on *bu gong zheng* meaning injustice and gave the whole translation as: *Zhe zhong bu gong zheng de xing wei bi xu ting zhi.* This injustice must stop. Wu Fan-zi nodded his head several times, then asked, "Which injustice must stop?"

Fong almost laughed but didn't – nothing remains funny for very long in a place that is beginning to stink of burnt human flesh.

"Crime Site Unit will want to go in first."

"So what else is new?" Wu Fan-zi lit a cigarette and carefully pocketed the match.

"I'll see what I can do about getting you in ahead of them."

Wu Fan-zi shrugged and headed out of the blast zone.

Lily stopped the Tibetan woman in the market. The woman smiled, revealing missing teeth and silver caps. Her dark eyes swam deep within her heavily wrinkled face. But she was not old. In fact, Lily couldn't tell whether the woman in front of her was older or younger than she.

"So – you back?"

The woman's Shanghanese was spotty, her breath formidable.

"I have returned as you can see," said Lily.

The Tibetan looked at Lily, then turned away.

Lily reached out and grabbed the woman's arm.

The Tibetan whirled quickly, reaching for her swolta blade as she did.

Lily almost screamed.

It was lucky for her that she didn't. "You back – I see – what want?"

Lily replied carefully, "You gave me photographs of some old statuary the last time."

"So, you buy or you think buy?" she asked sharply.

Lily wanted to see the pieces in the flesh but almost thought better of it when she saw the sun glint off the sharpness of the woman's knife.

"You, me follow."

And Lily did – through three densely packed alleys, then down a long set of steps into the sub-sub-basement of a building off Zhe Jiang Lu. Lily wasn't all that tall but even she had to lean forward to avoid banging her head against the ceiling in the dank sub-basement. The tiny Tibetan didn't need to bend. She flipped a switch. Three well-armed Tibetan men came to silent life.

"Pick, you," said the Tibetan woman, pointing to the ground.

Four lintel pieces were on the floor. Some were delicately carved, others had fresco paintings – all were sand-worn – ancient. And totally illegal.

"From the Taklamakan Desert," the Tibetan said. "Far west."

Lily knelt to get a better look. The first must have been a facing piece – perhaps the carved figures were family gods. The second was smaller and badly damaged. But there was a prize – a beautifully carved young boy. The third was obviously a vertical piece and seemed to depict a farming scene of some sort. The final one was also vertical. This had the standing figure of the man in ancient Western garb. He faced forward, his head looked slightly to his right, his palms turned upward. There was a beautiful calm to his face and lines of light radiated from his body.

Lily pointed to the fourth piece. Immediately, the Tibetan pulled out a hand calculator and punched in a very high number – what the Shanghanese call the laughing price. When you see that price, you are supposed to laugh. If you don't, then the merchant laughs – inside, of course.

Lily smiled – bartering was familiar territory. She chortled and then snapped the calculator out of the Tibetan's hands and punched in a ludicrously low figure – the crying price. The Tibetan shrieked in proper proportion to Lily's offer.

The bartering lasted twenty minutes. Lily threatened to leave twice, the Tibetan threatened to kill her once – just another day at the market.

Finally, a price was settled upon. Then Lily pressed the

Tibetans to deliver the object. "After all, a fine Han Chinese lady like myself cannot be seen parading through the streets with a piece of China's priceless history on her back."

A few more dickering moves and the delivery price was set.

Lily gave them the address of her office at the Hua Shan Hospital. They were to wrap the fresco and leave it with the receptionist down the stairs from her lab.

She insisted the object be well concealed and then asked, "When will it arrive?"

The Tibetan raised her shoulders.

"When?" Lily pressed.

"Within the week. We don't openly move objects of such value in the city. Shanghai's filled with thieves, you know." All of a sudden the woman's Shanghanese was perfect and her sense of irony very strong.

Lily gave them a 10-percent deposit and her very best I'm-a-cop-so-don't-fuck-with-me look.

As she left the Tibetans and stepped into the brilliant sunshine, she had a slight twinge – she'd just used her best cop look to do something illegal. Then she banished the thought from her head. Fong would love the piece and it would be their first present to Xiao Ming – their first- and only-born – on the occasion of her three-month birthday. It would also be the first of many purchases that were hers and Fong's – not Fong's and Fu Tsong's.

The heat in the operating room was still intense enough to mask the stink of death as Fong watched his "fireman's" eyes move – no, scan – the blasted-out surgery. Wu Fan-zi was almost half as wide as he was tall but not one ounce of him was fat. What little neck he had was substantially wider than his head. His muscular torso came directly from his Mongolian ancestry. He was basically a small building that had grown legs – and, oh yes, brains. Fong thought of Wu Fan-zi's expertise as the zen end of policing. He'd worked with Wu Fan-zi several times before his exile west of the Wall and each time he'd found it fascinating.

Wu Fan-zi horked up a wad of phlegm into his mouth but didn't spit it out. After all, this was a crime scene and there's no telling what stupid conclusion a CSU guy could come to if he found fresh phlegm on the floor. Wu Fan-zi had little patience with CSU guys – but then he'd been allowed into the crime site first this time – so he'd hold his phlegm. "Well?" Fong ventured.

Wu Fan-zi slowly brought his almost black eyes to meet Fong's gaze. Then he slid them past Fong and stared at a mass of tangled metal imbedded in the far wall.

"Well?" Fong ventured again.

Wu Fan-zi brought a handkerchief to his mouth and spat into it. "He's a pro – that's for sure."

Fong nodded. It wasn't something he hadn't figured out himself.

"Perhaps more advanced than we've ever seen, Fong."

That was new – and deeply troubling. "Great. We have enough trouble finding regular, old-fashioned, stupid arsonists." Arson was a relatively new crime in Shanghai.

"I'll need assistance and money to work on this properly."

"You'll have both," Fong assured him while he made a mental note that he'd never approached the new commissioner for money and should do some study before he stepped into that territory. "Where will you start?" Fong asked.

"With the mathematics of it," Wu Fan-zi said flatly. "We can find the weights of the surgical tables and can measure the flight patterns and the depth of penetration into the walls. We should be able to determine the resistance co-efficient of the building material in the wall. Plug all those numbers into the basic formula and at least we'll have an idea of the force released by the blast." He waved his ham-sized hand at the walls of the surgery. "From the force co-efficient we might be able to determine the type of explosive – might – no promises, Fong."

Fong nodded. Like in so much police work, a fireman's conclusions rested on a base of science but were highly influenced by intuition and supposition.

"Maybe we'll get lucky. If the force co-efficient . . ." he didn't bother completing the statement. The large man squatted down and put his hands on the concrete floor, palms down. It was hot to the touch. Then he leaned over and plucked a strand of thin metal wire from the floor. "Phosphorus," he muttered and looked away from Fong, clearly not interested in answering any questions. He approached the shattered window high up on the west wall. "I would have thought that surgeries wouldn't have windows," he said holding the strand of phosphorus in his palm.

Fong consulted the notes he'd been given by the hospital. "This is the newest operating theatre. It's only one of the two with windows." Fong looked to Wu Fan-zi. The man nodded but said nothing.

Fong waited. Finally, Wu Fan-zi turned to Fong. "Where will you begin?"

Fong pointed at the fetus in the cage, "With that."

"Why it didn't explode like the rest of the things in the room?"

"No, I'll leave that detail to you."

"How it got here then?"

"That and who put it there."

"I'm the head of administration for the People's Twenty-Second Hospital, Detective Zhong."

Fong immediately thought, "Not for long. Someone has to be blamed for this breach of security." Fong allowed himself to smile.

"I'm a busy man, sir!"

Fong wiped the smile from his face. He swallowed hard trying to keep anger out of his voice, but failed, "Busy?" It came out as a hiss.

"Yes, Inspector Zhong, busy," the man said, but his voice was unsure, wavering. "You wouldn't . . ."

"Too busy to help the police after an operating room in your hospital was blown to shit? That kind of too busy?"

"Well, no . . ."

Fong cut him off, "I want to interrogate the surgeons and their teams – the ones who were in the operating room before the explosion and those scheduled to go in after the blast. And I want to see the cleaners who swept up before and those ready to clean up after. I want an accurate roster count of those in the operating room at the time of the explosion. Also the name and address of all the women and their men folk who were in the waiting room." Before the man could protest, Fong added, "I need to compare body parts to names."

The man stiffened.

"And I want it within the hour – are you able to understand that? Good, now do you think you can 'administer' your way to getting that done?"

The surgery had cooled enough for the smell of burnt flesh to fill the air. Fong applied a thick stripe of tiger balm beneath his nose and inhaled deeply. His head snapped back from the sharp intake of the powerful eucalyptus odour. Then he pulled on his latex gloves, steeled himself, and entered the blasted-out surgery again.

The new head of the Crime Scene Unit looked up from his grisly task – one of his men was trying to lever a charred leg bone from a portion of the wall just above shoulder height. It was resisting his efforts – as if it had been disturbed enough for one day.

Fong had not worked with the new CSU guy before and wasn't sure how good he was. Fong had been spoiled in the past working with Wang Jun for years, before he was gunned down in the Pudong just before Fong was arrested and sent to internal exile.

Fong hadn't cared for the new man's behaviour in the commissioner's office, but he was willing to forget and forgive if the man were talented. But that remained to be seen. What was obvious was the man's caustic approach to his work. And that struck a wrong note in Fong.

The man dropped the bone fragment he was examining and looked at Fong. "You got the list?"

"Yeah."

The man held out his hand. Fong gave him the list. It contained the names of a doctor, three nurses, two technicians, and the patient, Ms. Wu. Beside each name was a basic physical description and home address and, in the case of the hospital workers, both blood type and DNA markers. China had, for years, been much further advanced in such research than they had ever acknowledged to the West.

The man spat.

Fong began to protest.

"What's the difference," the man said. "They're all dead. Grisly business they were involved in, anyway. Butchers butchered."

Fong couldn't believe it.

The man read the list quickly – then he pointed to several piles of bones, charred bits of clothing, seared flesh-covered body parts, teeth, and in one case a small pile of hair. "That's what's left of them."

Fong pointed at the hair but before he could speak the CSU responded, "Yeah, yeah, we can do DNA match from hair if we're lucky enough to find one with a follicle in place and you insist."

"I insist."

The man rose to his full height. He was considerably taller than Fong. Perhaps a Northener; definitely not a fan of Fong's.

"You're first on my list, but trust me they all must be here – none of these murderers escaped."

Fong controlled his anger and glanced at the piles – all that was left of seven lives and all the lives they could have created.

"No other hair was found but this?" asked Fong pointing to the small pile of hair.

"No other hair. Lots of bones and a fair number of teeth–"

"I want to know whose hair that is and fast." Fong began to leave, then stopped. "Where did you find the hair?"

The man riffled through a set of photographs. "On the floor under the surgical table."

"Near the fetus in the cage?" asked Fong, grabbing the photo.

"Yeah, beside a pool of blood – so?"

So, Fong didn't like it. He handed back the photograph and repeated even more sternly, "I want to know whose hair that is."

Fong noticed the CSU guy's eyes go past him. He turned. Lily was there in the doorway. Her beautiful eyes were moist with tears again. "What has happened here?" she asked in a small voice.

Fong was suddenly certain that she was going to faint. He moved quickly to her side and turned her away from the carnage.

"What has happened here?" she repeated.

"More to the point now, Lily, is 'who' has made this happen here?"

She looked into his eyes and he knew that she wanted him to comfort her but he walked her briskly away from the crime site. This was not a place for solace or sentiment. It was a place for cold calculation and thought.

Fong steered her back to the relative calm of the main reception area. "Are you all right, Lily?"

She nodded. But he was looking past her. One of his cops was standing beside a man dressed in some sort of black cassock.

Fong signalled the cop over to him. "Who's the ghoul?" Fong asked, a slow smile coming to his face.

"He's the bishop of Shanghai," said the cop as naturally as if he were saying that there is seldom very much chicken in an order of General Tzo's chicken.

"You're kidding. There's a bishop of Shanghai?"

"If there's a cathedral, there's a bishop."

"Well, there's a cathedral, that's true."

"Yes, sir, it's Xu Jia Hui Tian Zhu Jiao Tang on Caw Xi Lu. Have you ever been, sir, it's very nice?"

Fong caught something in the cop's voice. Something hurt, offended. He coughed into his fist to allow him a moment to remove the smile from his lips then said, "No I've never been to the cathedral."

"It's very nice, sir. It really is."

"I'm sure it is, but why is the bishop of Shanghai here?"

"I thought you wanted to see him."

"About what?"

"The cross you found in the old skeleton's throat?" He held out the cross in its evidence bag. Fong took it.

"Your timing's not so . . . No, yes, I mean you did fine. Thank you. Find me a private room and bring him."

Five minutes later, Fong entered a small office at the back of a forensics lab. The elderly, black-cassocked man stood in front of the desk. The cop stood to one side. Fong sat behind the desk and pointed to a chair. The man slowly sat, his back very erect. "Thanks for coming in, sir."

"Father," the man corrected Fong.

"What?"

"You may call me Father."

Before Fong could stop himself he snapped back, "I had a father."

"So did I," the man said, matching Fong's intensity.

"My father died a long time ago."

"During the fight for Liberation?"

"Yes, but how did . . .?"

"My father died in the same struggle," the man paused. "I'm not as old as I look."

There was a beat of silence after which Fong said, "If your father died in the Liberation he was a Communist like mine, so how did you . . .?" He didn't know the correct word so he waved his hand in the elderly man's direction.

The man's features softened. He didn't smile. "Some of us are chosen to make the leap to faith, my son."

"I'm not your son," Fong said.

"Fine. Some of us are chosen to make the leap to faith, Inspector Zhong."

Fong nodded then reached into his pocket and extracted the transparent evidence bag with the equal-sided crucifix. He held it out for the cleric to take, but the old man kept his hands in his lap. Fong offered it again, and again the man didn't take the cross.

"I'd prefer not to touch that, if you don't mind."

Fong thought, "I couldn't care less if you touch it."

Then the man spat out, "That's like a merchant hanging a sheep's head to sell dog meat."

"You'll blow a gasket like that," Fong thought but what he said was, "Fine, can you identify this piece of religious frippery?"

"There's no need to blaspheme!"

The man was initially pleased with the silence that his comment engendered, then he saw the cop behind him move so that he blocked any access to the door. He was at a complete loss. "What?" he asked.

Fong spoke very slowly, "I've never heard anyone use the

word *blaspheme* before. It's a very unique word."

"It's a very important word, Inspector Zhong."

"Worth dying for?"

The cleric was on his feet quickly.

"Sit down, sir," Fong said. The man quickly sat back in the chair. Fong held out the equal-sided cross. "Now, what is this?"

"An abomination."

Fong took a breath to control his temper then said, "An abomination of what?"

"Of our Lord's pain. His suffering. His resurrection. And of Mother Church."

"This little piece of metal is all those things? Quite a piece of metal, don't you think?"

"It's Manichaean, Inspector Zhong."

"And Manichaean would be what exactly?"

"A heresy."

Fong turned away from the man. Abomination, blasphemy, heresy – these folks have a way with the language. Fong drummed his fingers and without turning back said, "This was found deep in a man's throat. His neck bones were crushed around it." Fong turned back to the cleric. The man's face betrayed nothing.

"Perhaps because he was a heretic," the cleric said simply. Then he astonished Fong by quoting Mao's *Red Book* to back up his assertion, "If poisonous weeds are not removed, scented flowers cannot grow."

Fong ignored the quotation and pressed on. "So this may have been a religious murder? I mean it's possible he was killed because of this?"

"He may well have been killed because of what that thing stands for."

"Which is something that offends your church?"

"In matters of faith, my son, offend is much too mild a word to use."

CHAPTER SEVEN

THE INVESTIGATION BEGINS

The commissioner stood in the window of his office watching the moon set as Fong waited for the man to acknowledge his presence. When he finally turned he seemed oddly distracted.

There were two newspapers on his desk. One was the *New York Times,* the other the *Manchester Guardian.* Both had screaming headlines about the bombing in the People's Twenty-Second Hospital. Both quoted the arsonist's note in the cutline beneath a picture of the fetus in the cage.

The commissioner gestured toward the papers. "The last time the West paid so much attention to us, Mao was claiming to have swum across the Yangtze." His voice was light. Surprisingly breathy, as if he were about to faint.

Fong was tempted to quip back, "The good old days." But he thought better of it. He didn't know this man well enough to chance a jest. And the man's voice was frighteningly uncentred. So Fong said nothing. It'd been a long day and he was almost asleep on his feet.

"Tired, Inspector Zhong?" The voice was suddenly very high, almost falsetto.

Fong nodded, still unwilling to speak.

The commissioner pointed at the newspapers, "I really don't

care how long you've been awake or how many more days you need to go without sleep." Stabbing his finger at the cutline he barked out, "This outrage must stop!"

It took Fong a moment to realize that the man wasn't mocking the newspaper headline but giving an order. Fong checked a second time but there wasn't a trace of irony or sophistication in the liquid depths of the man's eyes. Just fear. A lot of fear.

"The year 2008 is not far away and the West is now watching us closely."

For a moment Fong couldn't figure out what 2008 had to do with an explosion in an abortion surgery. Then he remembered – the Olympics were going to be staged in Beijing in 2008. He smiled inwardly. Beijing must be up the man's ass so far that he could hardly breathe.

Fong hesitated. Desperate men were often difficult to approach but he didn't care. "My arson inspector needs more money to complete his investigation and we could use assistance from Hong Kong. They've had more experience with arson than we have."

For an instant he thought the man was going to scream at him but that passed.

"Fill out the forms and I'll sign them."

Fong nodded. That was easier than he had anticipated. Now let's go for broke he thought. "There's a young captain in Xian who helped me with the investigation into the murders on Lake Ching. I could use his assistance on this case . . . sir."

It seemed like the commissioner had either not heard or not understood. But just as Fong was about to repeat his request, the man said, "What's his name?"

The man's voice was suddenly sad.

Tough. We make our choices in this world and yours have led you to this dark place. Fong held no sympathy for those who rode the wave of politics when they were tossed broken and bleeding on the rocks.

"Chen. The man's name is Captain Chen."

Four hours later, at first light, a very young officer approached Fong at the entrance to Special Investigations. "The guy who found the note is here, sir. We let him spend the night at home."

"Fine. Where is he?"

"Interrogation Room 3."

Fong entered the room and stood to one side examining the young man. His eyes were a little too close together and there was a definite nastiness that was nearer the surface than he probably knew. He ought to learn to cover it better and damn soon, Fong thought.

Before Fong could speak, the man said, "I didn't see anyone. It's busy in the hospital, you know."

Fong said nothing, allowing the young man to simply sit in the silence. "Can I go now?"

That Fong answered: "No."

"Great, is this the silent treatment or something? You old guys are all the same. Where's your fucking Mao jacket – at the cleaners?"

Fong almost laughed out loud. This boy was playing the role he traditionally played. But Fong understood, although grudgingly, that he was now part of the old guard. Part of what was perceived by the young as holding the country back. It felt uncomfortable. Fong looked at the young man and decided on a tack. "So what did you want to be?"

"When I grew up?" he asked nastily.

"Sure," said Fong, "when you grew up."

"Not a fucking clerk in an abortion clinic, that's for sure."

"What then?"

"A doctor, if you must know."

"You're young enough still . . ."

". . . to do whatever I want. I know. You old guys always say shit like that."

"Do we?"

"Yes, you do." He looked to his left as if there were something or someone there who could help him. "What do you want from me, anyway?"

"I want to know how that note got on your desk?"

"I've told them already."

"I'm sure you did. Now tell me."

The receptionist let out a breath then sort of threw his hands up in the air in the universal gesture of when-will-this-nonsense-end. "Fine. I saw nothing. I saw no one in particular. The desk was a mad house. As usual. When I had a moment to myself I looked down and there was that piece of paper with the English writing on it."

"How did you know it was English?"

"I'm educated. I took primary English like everyone who wants to be anyone. So I recognized the letters – not their names – but that they were English."

Fong thought about that for a moment then asked, "How did you know they weren't German or French of Spanish?"

"Oh, very good, Inspector. You've caught me. I didn't know that. Can I go now?"

"Were there any Caucasians at the desk?"

The young man looked at him but didn't speak.

"Come on. You work at a Chinese hospital. Foreigners don't go there. Or if they did even a moron like you would remember it."

"Moron?"

"They never used to fight," Fong thought. But what he said was, "Yes, moron, now did you see any Caucasians or not that day?"

"No, I didn't."

"Very good."

"Thanks, asshole."

Fong looked at the man. "Do you really think I can't hurt you?"

"I don't care what you do to me."

That was new. Fong looked at the man and what he saw clearly on his face were the unmistakable signs of surrender. At his age he'd already given up. So young to have already lost hope. So young to be so angry. Fong gave him a card. "Call me if you remember anything more. There had to have been a Long Nose at your desk – as you said, the note's in English."

As a forensic scientist, Lily had dealt with many dead things – many mutilated things – many corroded, rotted, penetrated, scraped, cut, burned, strangled, scalded, blinded, poisoned things – but none of these had prepared her for interviewing the Hua Shan Hospital's abortion clinic's head nurse. She'd seen the heavy-set woman many times as she'd passed by the clinic and gone up the stairs to her lab. But before today they'd never exchanged any more than cursory greetings.

The woman shrugged toward a chair in her small office. Lily sat. The nurse stood. "My supervisor says you have questions for me, officer."

Lily did her best to smile, then said, "I do."

"About the bombing?"

"Not directly. I need to understand more about abortion ORs."

"Fine," the nurse said curtly, "the clinic is filling up, so please be quick."

Lily didn't like the woman's tone but that made things equal. Clearly, the woman didn't like Lily's very presence in her office.

The woman quickly went over the basic scheduling of an abortion surgery – the time involved on the table, prep times, clean-up regimes, etc. When she finished, she looked at Lily, "Anything else?"

"In the bombing, a human fetus was found . . ."

". . . in a cage. Yes, I heard."

"It had to have come from somewhere."

"Clearly."

"Could it have come from your surgery?"

That seemed to put the nurse back on her stubby heels. When she found her voice it was not nearly so assured as before, "How would I know?"

Lily's head quickly filled with a terrible image. She forced it aside and asked, "Is an inventory kept?"

"Of what?"

"Of . . . the product."

The head nurse looked as if she'd been asked if she'd visited Mars lately. Finally, she said, "No. No inventory is kept."

"So what do you do with . . .?" Lily couldn't find the word she wanted – or was willing to use.

The nurse nodded and said simply, "The detritus? What do we do with the detritus?"

"Yes," Lily answered, aware that the nurse had helped her. "Thank you," Lily said.

The nurse nodded and then said, "Nothing very sophisticated, officer. If the 'product' is big enough – if it can't be flushed – we double-bag it and it goes out with the hospital's trash. It's the same at all the hospitals, I expect."

Lily thought about the constant comings and goings of trash collectors. She had no idea where garbage eventually went – incinerated she guessed. But she suspected that whoever took this detritus didn't wait til the final drop point. She knew it wouldn't be difficult to don a garbage collector's overalls and pick up the refuse from one of the many abortion clinics around town as long as you were Chinese, but things here pointed toward an American.

"Has your clinic received any threats?"

"No."

"Have there been any Caucasians around the clinic?"

"Not that I've ever seen."

"This is my card . . ."

"I know where to find you if I need you, Lily." The woman turned and headed out to the crowded, angry waiting room.

Lily watched the woman go and wondered how she managed to deal with so much sorrow on a daily basis.

Fong looked around the conference room. They already appeared as tired as he felt. A folder was open in front of Wu Fan-zi; the new head of CSU was to his left. Six detectives were seated around the room completing their interview notes. Lily sat to one side, sipping from a steaming jar of cha. Her exhaustion carved deep patterns on her face making her look severe, stern. Fong knew she'd rushed home yesterday to settle Xiao Ming in for a night with her mother and then returned to the lab to get ready for the meeting. He didn't know about her early morning meeting with the head nurse of the Hua Shan Hospital's abortion clinic.

All eyes slowly turned to Fong, and what little chatter there had been in the room died.

The silence that followed was rife with possibilities. Everyone at the large oval table knew that this was Fong's first big case since his return from west of the Wall and his still shadowy success at Lake Ching. In the corridors of Special Investigations these events were collectively referred to as The Resurrection. Everyone also knew that there were many in the department anxious to see Fong fall on his delicately boned face.

The meeting room smelled of pungent cigarette smoke. Fong instinctively reached for his pack of Kents. But they weren't there. He hadn't smoked since he'd killed the assassin Loa Wei Fen in the construction pit in the Pudong. Fong cleared his throat and tossed two newspapers onto the large oval table. Instantly he was flooded with a memory of another time. Another newspaper he'd tossed on this very table. That newspaper's headline had screamed: Dim Sum Killer at Large. Of course that had been over five years ago. Back when he still smoked Kents.

Lily's voice cracked his reverie with her slightly lisped English, "Talk time, short stuff."

That reminded Fong of yet another time – another table – another investigation. He smiled at his wife, then asked in English, "How's our little girl?"

"Mother mine with. Miss you, though," Lily replied in English.

Fong wanted to reply, "No. She misses you, Lily," but didn't when he saw a darkness cross the new CSU guy's face. This was a multiple murder investigation, not a family gathering. Fong straightened his jacket, reminded himself that he had to lead all of them, not just Lily. As if he could ever really lead Lily! He turned to Wu Fan-zi, his fireman, and said in Mandarin, "You're up."

The block-like man looked haggard as he shuffled his papers. He opened his mouth then decided something or other and closed it. He smiled for no discernible reason, then said, "I've had to ask for help on this one. With Fong's permission I sent my preliminary results to Hong Kong and they've responded with an initial critique. But they don't want to work at a distance from the investigation."

"What does that mean?" asked Lily drily.

Fong sighed, then said, "They want one of their people on the investigation team."

"Well, they can't have it," snapped Lily.

Despite the People's Republic of China's takeover of Hong Kong, most of the officers around the table had been raised on a steady diet of hatred for the old English Protectorate.

"They can't insist on being a part of this investigation, can they, Fong?" Lily asked.

"They can and I've already arranged for them to send over their man."

Turning away from Lily's angry face, he returned to Wu Fan-zi, "What've you got so far?"

Wu Fan-zi went through the complex mathematics of the blast. They all listened carefully. Finally Wu Fan-zi stopped reciting numbers and said simply, "It was a very strong, very controlled bomb – unlike anything we've seen here. It's sophisticated in both its components and its execution. Only its detonation was simple. Then," he said, "there's this." He took out a plastic evidence bag and emptied out three short metal threads on the table. "Phosphorus threads," he said. "They were around the table – in a circle. Obviously those that ignited we don't have, although we were able to spot several that had only partially burned. The pattern is clear. A circle around the operating table." He pushed his chair away from the table and looked at Fong. "Phosphorus makes no sense. It couldn't be part of the bomb but it must have been scattered by the bomber. The threads are small enough that I doubt any-one working in the operating room would have noticed them."

"So, is there a question here, Wu Fan-zi?" asked Fong.

"Why would he bother, Fong? Phosphorus converts energy into light so quickly that it hardly gives off any heat at all. There's almost no force released because all the energy is imme-diately converted into high intensity light."

"So the phosphorus has nothing to do with the bomb?" Fong asked.

"Not as far as I can tell," replied Wu Fan-zi.

Fong thought, "Maybe nothing to do with the bomb but def-initely something to do with the bomber," but all he chose to say was, "Okay. Let's leave the phosphorus for now. Could the bomb have been purchased here?" asked Fong.

Wu Fan-zi thought about that then nodded. "Yeah, it could if you have the money and the contacts. It's rare that a white man could be so well connected in the Middle Kingdom. Shit, even if Silas Darfun were alive today he'd have a tough time getting his hands on that stuff."

The others gave short chortles, not real laughs.

"What we do know is that the bomb isn't homegrown. We've got a pretty tight lid on all that. Government stockpiles are cross-checked constantly and it's almost impossible to get the kind of materials necessary to make that kind of bomb here. Just try buying a large amount of bicarbonate of soda and watch what happens. The Internet sites are all monitored and all hits are traced. Hey-ka-ka-ka-kaboom.com seems to be the biggest but there's seldom anything they get by us. The site has, in fact, been extremely cooperative – don't ask me why. Besides, even if you ordered something from the Internet it still has to be delivered and we have that covered too. So that leaves us with an importer. My guess is the bomb came across the Russian frontier. But I doubt if it was Russian. They were never very clever with explosives. They always left that to the Czechs."

"And the Bosnians," added the CSU guy.

"True," Wu Fan-zi responded.

"But it would still be so much easier to find this explosive in the West – and the note was in English, wasn't it?" asked the CSU guy.

Fong ignored the question but asked one of his own: "Would it be hard to smuggle the bomb through airport security, Wu Fan-zi?"

"Yeah." Wu Fan-zi wasn't about to supply any more information on that topic but his terse answer bespoke inside knowledge.

"Hard or impossible?" Fong prodded.

"Impossible, Fong."

The CSU guy looked away as Wu Fan-zi continued, "And the detonator, the timing device, the metal cage – all that couldn't be smuggled in either. So it would all have to be obtained locally."

"So the bomber's entire kit would have to be bought here?"

"Yep," said Wu Fan-zi, "maybe not homegrown but definitely home bought."

Fong turned to one of the detectives, "Start with the cage the baby was–"

"Not a baby, Fong." Lily's voice was icy cold. In English she continued, "Xiao Ming is baby. This not."

Fong quickly translated to the men around the table. He saw clearly that they were not interested in the difference that Lily was pointing out. Lily saw their resistance and slammed her hand, palm down, on the table and then said loudly in English, "Important, this!"

Fong both understood and didn't understand what Lily was so upset about but now was not the time to explore it further. He looked past his wife and pointed to the young detective at her side. "Start with the cage. Someone made that thing. I want to know who."

The young man nodded. Fong handed him a photograph of the cage, sans fetus, and a piece of paper. "Here are the specs." He turned to Wu Fan-zi. "What's that metal called again?"

"Titanium," said the fireman.

"Is that why it didn't shatter – being made of this titanium metal?" asked the young detective.

"That and its position beneath the base of the steel surgical table," said Wu Fan-zi, then added, "and of course there was the planch."

"The what?"

"The planch. This is all that's left of it," Wu Fan-zi said, putting a badly dented very thick piece of metal plate on the table. "Some explosives can be given directionality by shaping the material. But it's a crude method and not totally reliable. The placement of the planch adds to the accuracy. The planch forces the energy of the explosion up and out."

"Away from the thing in the cage," said Lily.

"Away from the message in the cage," Fong corrected her none too gently.

There was another silence, then Fong barked at the young detective, "Go!" The man quickly headed toward the door. Before he got there Fong added, "I want an update on my desk by noon tomorrow." The man stopped, went to protest, then thought better of it as he noted the grim set of Fong's face.

He left, slamming the door harder than was absolutely necessary to close it.

"Another happy camper," Lily said in English.

Fong's textbook English couldn't decipher the meaning of the phrase. Why was Lily inferring that the detective could be hitched to the back of an automobile or for that matter that the man was happy?

Fong put aside these questions and turned to the CSU guy. He nodded his head. The man began his report, "All the people in the operating room left identifiable remains. The doctor, the technicians, the–"

"Who did the hair belong to?" Fong demanded.

The CSU guy checked his notes. "The head nurse."

"And the pool of blood?"

"Hers as well but I don't–"

Fong cut him off again, "Nothing else from the head nurse? No bones? No body parts? No teeth?" Fong was speaking fast, clearly angry.

"None," said the CSU guy slowly.

"But there were bones and body parts, teeth, and clothing from all the others?"

"Yes, we found–"

"Find her," Fong shouted.

Instantly there was chaos in the room. Cries of protest and anger over the apparent disrespect for the dead. Fong allowed the anger to crest, then as it began to fall he said simply, "She's not dead. You three, find her." He was pointing to a group of detectives. "Here," he said tossing the hospital administrator's data sheet onto the table. "Use this to start." Then he turned to the window. As one of the detectives took the sheet the other two quickly compared notes with the new CSU man. Then the three detectives headed out. They made no effort to hide the fact that they were happy to leave the room. Once the detectives were gone, Fong turned back to the CSU guy.

Lily had never seen Fong so angry. His words came out as little more than a hiss, "Leave your notes. You're off the case."

The man glared at Fong then left the room quickly. Lily turned to Fong but before she could ask her question he spoke to those remaining in the room, "There was no way to miss the fact that the hair and blood must have been planted there. He didn't want to know. He thought the people in that abortion surgery got what they deserved."

After a moment of silence one of the remaining detectives said, "Abortion is still a complicated subject."

Fong felt himself enveloped in dizziness, a world spinning. Fu Tsong, his first wife, dead in his arms, their unborn child on her belly. A yawning pit beneath them. Oh yes, Fong knew that abortion is a complicated subject. He knew that.

He caught Lily's sidelong look. No. He would not share the death of his first wife with her. "Forensics," he snapped.

Lily took the note that had been left behind. It had been carefully dusted then resealed in the evidence bag: THIS BLAS-PHEMY MUST STOP.

Fong translated the messages for the men around the table. "What is blasphemy?"

"I'll explain later. Tell us what you found on the note, Lily."

"The paper is pretty standard issue bond paper. Made here. Probably in the new factory across the river in the Pudong. But there's nothing to follow up there. The note is clean of fingerprints except for a thumb and forefinger of the guy at hospital reception. The lack of other fingerprints is rare since paper is such a good medium for prints. The ink is from a cheap disposable pen much like Fong uses. The words – are the words." She shrugged. "I know it's not much but it's all I've got on that."

She pushed forward the titanium cage. "The cage was fabricated recently and with a high level of skill. Titanium is hard to work with and the welding joints can be complicated because they need such high heat. The bars are almost exactly symmetrical and the base is nearly a perfect circle. No prints. No fabric or hair traces. Not much to go on really but I'll get a copy of this to the investigating detective." She reached for the two newspapers on the table. "Both papers have stringers in Shanghai but there are no credits given for either the stories or the pictures. As well, there is no way of telling if the picture is of the actual cage that we found. Personally I doubt it."

"How could the papers get the pictures, Lily?"

"They could have been dropped off with the stringers but we've checked. They both deny it. Both also deny they wrote the story. They claim the story and picture arrived at their head office in America by e-mail before the bomb went off. When the stringers confirmed the facts of the blast, their papers ran the story. There is no traceable e-mail traffic from the Middle Kingdom to these newspapers so we have to assume the e-mail came from somewhere else. This bomber could have an accomplice or he could have set his computer in America to send e-mails on a certain day to certain papers."

"Can e-mail do that?"

"If you have the right software it's no problem."

"How about these stringers?"

"What about them?"

"You believe these guys – these stringers – Lily?"

"I do. They're both old China hands. They both have good reason to want to stay here and therefore play by the rules."

"And the reason they want to stay here, Lily?"

"One is married to a Chinese girl, the other has a weakness for Chinese women."

"Ah."

"Ah, indeed, Fong." Lily smiled at her own cleverness.

"Is that all, Lily?" Fong prompted her in English.

She shot him a hard look. "Not all, Fong, and it know you!" she retorted angrily in her version of English. Her hands trembled as she opened a small transparent folder. She put on a pair of reading glasses. She didn't look up as she read the Mandarin characters. Her voice was soft – distant – so un-Lily-like.

"The fetus was of a seven-month-old male. Two pounds three ounces. Han Chinese. It seems to have been partially mummified. Perhaps by the blast. No matching DNA markers with known suspects or other victims. No way to tell how long ago it died–" She stopped, realizing the implication of what she had just said. If it had died it must at one time have been alive. She shook her head. Fong was frightened she might break into tears. She didn't. "The fetus was wrapped in a flame-retardant metal sheathing with an asbestos lining – industrial strength, easy enough to find at any construction site. The lining, that is. The metal was titanium." She turned the page and continued to read. It took five more minutes for her to complete her report – all very dry, very accurate – pretty much useless and she knew it. She closed the folder and reached for her tea. When she brought the steaming liquid to her lips her glasses misted over. It hid the tears in her eyes.

Fong allowed a moment of silence, then said, "Find out what the hospital does with discarded fetuses." No one moved. No one wanted that assignment.

"They flush them or throw them in the garbage," said Lily, her voice thickening. "I checked this morning assuming that none of the men around this table would mind if I did this part of the investigation."

"Thanks, Lily," he said in English.

"Hey, please aim do I."

"Right," Fong thought but said nothing to her. He turned away from her. "You," he said pointing to the nearest cop, "find the route between the People's Twenty-Second Hospital and the nearest incinerator. It may even be in the hospital. Now."

"Fine," said the cop getting to his feet. He strode to the door and pushed it open. A muffled "ouch" came from the other side. A stubby rat of a man poked his head around the door and smiled when he saw Fong. Then he saw Lily and he positively beamed.

Lake Ching's Captain Chen had come to the big city.

CHAPTER EIGHT

THAT NIGHT

ily and Fong took Chen out for dinner that night in the Old City. Even as they walked toward the restaurant Fong wondered if Chen was going to get along in Shanghai. He was such a rube! He kept bobbing around to take in the sights. It made him bump into person after person – a definite no-no on Shanghai's constantly packed streets.

Chen apologized profusely in his country accent to each and every person with whom he collided. But Shanghanese are not good at accepting apologies from their country cousins and many retorted with intensely unkind descriptions of the poor man. Fortunately for Captain Chen, most of the slanders were spat out in such furiously fast and extremely idiomatic Shanghanese that it was hard for him to understand. Lily and Fong shouted back at Chen's assailants until Chen stopped them. "Even the cat may look at the king," he quoted.

Fong was pretty sure this expression referred to the rights of the lowly to view their superiors, and in the realms of beauty Chen was far from being king.

As they passed by the Jade Buddha Temple, Chen stopped. "Can I go in?"

Fong had never been inside the popular tourist attraction that was supposed to be the "home" of the city god. "Sure," he said.

Inside the temple, the city seemed to slip away amid the quiet and the wafting smell of incense. Chen paid for six long sticks, knelt on the low rest in front of one of the large statues, then set the incense alight. As he bowed his head he rubbed the sticks slowly between his palms.

Fong and Lily stood to one side. Fong looked around. Tourists with camcorders were everywhere. For a moment it occurred to Fong that it was wrong to take pictures in places like this, then he cast the thought aside. Why not, it was just a building set aside to honour superstition. He glanced back at Chen. The young man swayed slightly while he recited his prayers. As he did, it seemed to Fong that a remarkable transformation took place – the overriding clunkiness of Captain Chen gave way to an undeniable elegance. Something about the rhythm of the man's silent recitation lent him a kind of grace.

Fong stepped outside. The whole "thing" of the place made him feel uncomfortable. The term *left out* came to him but he dismissed it. For the first time in a very long time he intensely craved a cigarette.

Chen came out shortly, with Lily at his side. Both were smiling. Fong led the way through the dank realities of the Old City. They entered a restaurant and Chen marvelled at the choices available on the menu.

"Order what you like, Chen, this is on us," Lily said.

"Thank you, Miss Lily . . . or is it Mrs. Zhong?"

"For you Lily is fine . . . no Miss. Just Lily," she smiled at him and touched his hand.

Fong wondered what had happened to Chen's wife who he had once described as "a sad woman who can't get pregnant and blames me." By the time Fong had figured out what was behind the grotesque murders on the lake boat on Lake Ching, and he and Lily were ready to leave Xian, Chen wasn't talking about his wife at all. They had probably separated, Fong thought. Why not? Chen was young – almost exactly Lily's age. He had lots of time to find someone new.

"Food good, Captain Chen?"

"Great, sir. Aren't you going to eat, sir?"

Fong sipped his Tzing Tao beer and said, "I'm not hungry. Are you ready to work?"

"That's why I'm here . . . sir," Chen said, catching a live shrimp between his chopsticks and plunking it into his mouth.

"Fine. I want you to lead the investigation into who made this." Fong took out a photograph of the metal cage in which the fetus had been found. Chen looked closely at the image then put down his chopsticks and spat out the shrimp. He suddenly wasn't hungry either.

A half-mile north of where Fong, Lily, and Chen sat, Robert stared at Tuan Li across a cheap card table. They were on Good Food Street down by the river. The street was closed to traffic nightly and turned into the world's largest outdoor restaurant. It was one of Tuan Li's favourite places. It was hardly classy dining and Robert knew he stood a very good chance of being quite sick the next morning – but Tuan Li was worth it.

"There was an explosion in the city today," she said.

"I heard."

"In a hospital. Awful."

He nodded but thought, "Politics. None of my fucking business."

A waiter plunked down a dish of steaming noodles in front of Tuan Li. She quickly swirled the sauce into the noodles and wrapped a swath around her chopsticks. "Open," she said extending the noodles toward Robert's mouth.

"This wouldn't be *traif*, would it?" he mocked.

"Is that one of those kosher things?" she mocked back.

Robert wanted to say, "Yes, it's one of those kosher things," but his mouth was filled with the thick noodles. They tasted glorious but he knew that often the company made the food taste better than it actually was. He recalled a particular croissant after a particular night with a particular dark-haired Montrealer. Then he couldn't believe he was reminiscing about another woman with Tuan Li across the table from him making bedroom eyes. What the fuck was wrong with him!

"Nice trip?" Tuan Li asked as a small sad smile came to her lips.

"How do you mean?" Robert covered, surprised that she could see through him so easily.

"You're not nearly as good a liar as you think, Robert."

"I'm sorry to disappoint you in my . . ."

"It must be very lonely where you are, Robert," she stated flatly. "Do you know why your mind floats like that?"

"No. Do tell."

"Because you have no faith. No faith. No love."

Robert thought, "No trust. No love," but said nothing.

"You know that play I'm working on?"

"The one about the dumb nigger?"

"You are a very bad person," she said. "The love in that play exists because of faith. Both Othello and Desdemona know that love is the gift the gods bring after you make the leap to faith. But no leap to faith. No falling in love."

"Well, it doesn't exactly work out – the love in this play."

"No. True. But they have at least lived. Known each other."

"I've 'known' you in the biblical sense," Robert shot back.

"No. Robert. We've contacted each other but we have not known each other – in the biblical or any other sense."

"Well, maybe that's all there is – contacting each other."

"Maybe there's more, Robert, and you just refuse to see it. You have been with a lot of women but have found no place to rest."

He sighed deeply. "You want to go on with this?"

Tuan Li canted her elegant head, "I do. How long have you been like this?"

"Always," he said, hoping that would end the conversation on that topic.

"You were always like this?" Tuan Li prodded.

"Yes, I've always been like this."

"I don't believe it."

"It's true."

"When did you first experience this? Be honest, Robert."

"When I was a kid. My parents sent me to summer camp. Jewish people in Toronto always sent their kids to summer camps named after trees – don't ask me why."

"Why, Robert?"

"I thought I asked you not to . . ."

"You did. Why?"

"Well, probably because there are lots and lots of trees – trees, trees, trees, and one Succoni station. Lenny Bruce said that – heard of him?"

"No. Why do you do that?"

"Do what?

"Talk fast about things that don't matter?"

"Because . . ."

"Yes, I'm listening."

"Because I've almost always done that." Before she could jump on top of the "almost" he continued, "At any rate I remember coming home from a tree camp by train and getting off with all the other campers and going into the central hall of Union Station. It's the downtown train station – not nearly as big as your North Train Station – but plenty big for a kid. Well, everywhere there were kids hugging parents. I looked around and couldn't find my folks. A neighbour was there and she told me to wait with her. She saw I was upset and she held out her arms to me. I hugged her. It didn't matter to me that she wasn't my mother. I hugged her because I needed to be hugged and it really didn't matter to me who she was. Because it was just as fucking good with this woman as with my mother." He blushed. He hadn't intended to spit all that out. He burbled a laugh, then dismissed his outburst with, "Any port in a storm I guess."

"But there is no storm here, Robert."

"You're sure about that?"

"Yes I am, Robert. I know what a storm is – and I sense that you do too. But you won't share what you know with me." She waited but he did not speak. Finally she said, "I cannot love a man who cannot fall in love. And you cannot fall in love unless you make the leap of faith to believe in love despite the storms that might be there. What are you doing in Shanghai, Robert? Don't think about your answer, just answer."

Robert said nothing. How could he tell her that he was "antiquing" to raise money so he could investigate a crime that may or may not have happened over fifty years ago. A crime that may or may not have ruined his life.

She shook her head and took a deep breath. "I hope your secrets can keep you warm, Robert." She put her napkin on the table, touched her fingers to his face, then stood.

He watched her disappear into the omnipresent crowd that is Shanghai, not noticing that she passed within a hair's breath of a man who had been staring at them. A man from Virginia called Angel Michael by his associates but named Matthew by his adoptive father.

Matthew watched Tuan Li's departure. He knew that she was considered beautiful, even exquisite by some. For the first time in his life he wished he understood that – no he wished that he saw that. He had succeeded in the first step of his plan – succeeded brilliantly – and now he wanted to reward himself. But with what? The food in front of him could have been diced cardboard for all the joy it gave him. For that matter, Tuan Li could have been a deformed old crone for all the thrill he got from looking at her.

He turned in his seat and noticed that his hands were

shaking. Quickly the familiar wave of pain began to form behind his left eye. He reached into his pocket and pulled out a pack of stick matches. He managed to get one out and snap its head against a thumbnail. It flared – and the pain backed off. His hands stopped shaking.

Suddenly a long thin cigarette was thrust into the flame's brightness.

Matthew looked up.

"Light me," said the whore.

Matthew snuffed out the light and glared at her.

"Hey, it's your loss, puny one," she hissed as she turned and left. But as she told her girlfriend later that night, "I got the chills. It's like that bastard froze my heart."

Fong couldn't sleep. Chen was camped on the tiny couch in their small apartment on the Shanghai Theatre Academy's campus. He snored. "Naturally he would snore," Fong thought as he looked out the window. Three young male actors were drunkenly lounging on the lawn by the Henry Moore-esque statue. Fong noted their faces. All would be the only children their families would ever have. For the briefest moment Fong wondered how many had been "selected" by their parents.

Chen snorted loudly and pulled the blanket up to his lantern jaw.

Fong moved over to the crib. Xiao Ming slept on her back – her pudgy hands slowly clenching and unclenching in response to some secret nocturnal vision.

Fong reached down and gently touched his daughter. She momentarily wakened and looked at him full in the face. She was so present. So there. He'd heard that boy children spent about a year slowly coming into the world. But he had found that Xiao Ming had been aware of everything from the very beginning.

He smiled. She watched his features move and tried to imitate them. She got close, but a few muscle groups misfired and she ended up with an oddly quizzical look on her face.

Fong knew he should be happy. He was back in Shanghai. He had been reinstated as head of Special Investigations. He had a child. Yes, he should be happy. But something nagged at him. Pulled him toward a waiting darkness. Fong lifted Xiao Ming and held her head against his shoulder. He felt her breath on his neck – it was soft, soft, and so warm. A sweetness from far away. He held her out at arm's-length. She looked away from him. The darkness drew his eyes to the wall mirror. There they were, as if captured in the glass. He noted the distance between them. An arm's-length. A shiver went through him. Something about their relative positions. He continued holding her at arm's-length and knelt.

He put Xiao Ming on the floor and turned away. Then he looked back at her. How had the baby's skull been positioned in the construction pit? Away. She had been looking away from her father. At least the killers had allowed that. At least the last image in the baby's mind would not be the agony of the ritual murder of her father. Fong allowed his head to loll back and opened his throat as far as he could. How great the fear would have to be to make a man swallow his own crucifix. He held Xiao Ming's hand tightly as if saying goodbye.

"Fong!"

Lily snatched Xiao Ming from the floor. "How could you, Fong? This is our baby. Not an old skull buried in the ground! What are you thinking! Really, Fong. What are you thinking?" She turned with Xiao Ming in her arms and hurried into their bedroom, slamming the door behind her.

Fong hung his head. "You're right, Lily. What am I thinking?"

"You scared me," said the head nurse of the abortion surgeries at the People's Twenty-Second Hospital when Angel Michael entered the room he had rented for her.

"Did I?" asked Matthew as he took out the even-sided cross and handed it to her.

As she took the icon she turned from him. The wide patch of missing hair exposed the nape of her neck. Matthew had read that the nape of a woman's neck is very erotic. He looked at the back of the nurse's neck but saw nothing but slack sinew and aging flesh.

She turned back to him. The cross now hung directly beneath her Adam's apple. "Would you like a drink to celebrate our glorious start?"

He looked at the woman before him. "*Our* glorious start?" he thought. But all he said was, "That cross suits you."

CHAPTER NINE

AND IN AMERICA

There was palpable anger in the air of the over-air-conditioned room in Virginia. Copies of the *New York Times* and several other papers were spread on the table. All screamed of death and mayhem in a Shanghai abortion clinic – and, of course, of the fetus in a cage.

"This is completely beyond what we agreed to," said Larry, a tall, thin, Yale-ish man.

There were loud expressions of agreement around the table.

"This was a slaughter."

"Jesus! What was Angel Michael thinking of?"

"God," said the older man, who Angel Michael called his father. That silenced the room. The white-haired man looked at the last speaker, "And I'd remind you that it's a sacrilege to use His name in vain."

"Yes, but so many dead!"

"A hundred dead, two hundred, five hundred. That place murders a thousand beings every week – year after year," snapped back the older man. "What are those dead to the fifty thousand killed every year? This is a war. I warned you when we started. I warned you that this wouldn't be simple. But there is a simple reality that we all must face. Mid-term Congressional elections are approaching and not a single candidate in this country has even mentioned abortion. Not one has come out against the slaughter of babies. We have to put the evil of abortion back in the light where it belongs. That's why we're here. That's what we are doing."

"Yes, but–"

"But nothing. The sword is in Angel Michael's hand – we put it there. All of us here did that. And we know why we did it."

Eyes were averted around the table.

"Lest anyone have second thoughts now – I've had all our conversations in this room videotaped." Before the uproar could start, he continued, "There's no going back. In the eyes of the law we are all accessories to multiple murder – a crime punishable by death in Mr. Bush's America."

"That'll shut them up for a while," the older man who Matthew called his father thought. As the truth of the situation sank into the minds of the people around the table he allowed his thoughts to drift to Angel Michael. Such a big first step and so melodramatic – the fetus in the cage. So gaudy. So unlike the boy he had carefully raised as his son – his weapon to return the world to God. He looked out the window at the setting sun, at the quiet beauty of the Virginia farm country. Then for the first time in his life he questioned the wisdom of his plan, the wisdom of putting the sword in Angel Michael's hand.

Later that night, after he read the reports more closely, he had a second question about Angel Michael. Where did the boy he raised as his son get the money necessary to pull off such a feat?

* * *

The arrival the next morning of a large unmarked package at the reception desk of the Hua Shan Hospital set alarms ringing all over Shanghai. Fong raced out of his apartment still wet from a shower meant to fool his body into believing that it had slept well. He ran past the academy's theatre in which *Othello* was being rehearsed. Out the gate and down Ya'nan Lu to the Hua Shan Hospital. People streamed out of the hospital complex as the sound of approaching sirens filled the air. A tourist with a video camera taped the proceedings.

The local block wardens stepped aside as Fong approached them. The head of hospital security ran over to him, "A large unmarked package arrived at reception, sir."

"Has anyone touched it?"

"No, I immediately had the lobby cleared and started the evacuation of the hospital wards."

"Then you called me?"

"Right, sir."

"Fine. Call my office and get the arson division over here."

"It's already been done," said Wu Fan-zi as he moved toward Fong while putting on the last of the bomb protection gear.

Fong took him by the arm and guided him to the top of the steps leading into the Hua Shan Hospital's front entrance. "You take a good look?"

"Only a peak. It's big."

"Does that mean it's powerful?"

"Not necessarily. In fact, it makes no sense for a bomb to be that big."

"Then why get into the suit?"

"I'm fifty-two, right?"

"If you say so."

"Well, I am and next year I'd like to be fifty-three."

Wu Fan-zi turned and looking like something that could walk on the moon entered the front door of the Hua Shan Hospital.

Fong moved down the steps to the front row of the gathering crowd and waited with everyone else. Then he felt flesh press into his hand. He looked to his left. Lily was at his side, her fingers intertwining with his.

"A bomb, Fong?" Lily asked in English.

"I don't know. Wu Fan-zi is in there now."

"Everyone out?"

"Everyone who can safely be moved is out or in the process of getting out. Most are in the back courtyard."

"From bomb far enough?"

"We think so, Lily," Fong said, still speaking English.

The young man standing to one side was surprised by the crowd on the hospital steps and even more surprised to see the delicately boned middle-aged man speaking English to the younger woman beside him. He heard the wail of sirens and saw more cops arrive. Something had clearly gone wrong. They couldn't have found the cage already and the fully wired bomb was still in the briefcase he carried at his side – the message in an envelope in his left hand.

What had gone wrong? He mentally retraced his steps that day. It had been a little more complicated to get the cage with its grisly contents into position. More complicated without the assistance of a nurse, but not impossible – just a little climb. Surely they hadn't already found the cage. Not yet. If not, then why is the place swarming with cops?

He could have placed the bomb at the same time as the cage if his explosives supplier hadn't suddenly doubled the price and demanded cash – but he had. Then another thought occurred to him and he almost swore. He thought about the e-mails queued and ready to be sent to newspapers throughout the Western world. Then he sighed. There was no way to stop them now without making contact with his remote server and he knew that contact could be traced back to him.

A setback, but not a disaster. All around him police officers were readying themselves. "For nothing," he thought. Then he remembered the note he was carrying in his left hand. He knew he should get rid of it.

He surveyed the scene before him. For a moment he considered abandoning his briefcase and its incriminating contents, but the explosive snuggled there had cost him a small fortune to obtain. He looked back at the middle-aged Chinese man who had been speaking English. A cop? Maybe. Then his eyes went to the younger woman at his side. Her gaunt features struck an odd note in him. "Was he responding to her beauty?" he wondered. Then he saw her sad eyes and he almost gasped aloud – they were filled with light. For the first time in many, many years he had a yearning to reach out and touch flesh that was not his own.

She turned and looked right at him. His heart skipped a beat – then another. Her eyes moved past him. He had a terrible desire to tell the lady with the light in her sad eyes not to worry – that it was only he, Angel Michael, bringing back the light.

Chen introduced himself to the two detectives who had started tracking down the origins of the titanium cage. He hadn't gotten out more than an awkward hello before a familiar grin crossed the faces of the two men. Chen allowed a beat to pass then asked them to present the work that they had done so far. After an initial resistance they presented their preliminary findings because they quickly recognized two things: Fong and Lily were this guy's personal backers, and this ugly young man with the country manners and peasant accent was a talented cop.

Chen was happy that it hadn't taken too long to win the men over. He knew there was much work to do and that Fong was counting on him. He asked to see the actual cage. The men unwrapped the thing and put it on the table.

Chen stared at the titanium structure. The idea of the fetus in the thing left an indelible image in his mind. It was in fact his inability to implant such a thing in his wife's womb that had led to the ignominious end of their six-year marriage. He had been lucky to have her even that long – everyone had said so.

Even his mother had agreed when he told her of the divorce.

Divorce was not complicated in China but it was highly frowned upon. Divorce in the countryside, where Chen lived, started with a trip to the county seat where the estranged husband and wife had to undergo counselling from a party representative. The advice, often a directive, was invariably to stay together. However, when Chen arrived with his wife, the party representative, a busybody old lady, took one look at him and said to his wife, "How long have you been married?"

"Six years," Chen's wife replied.

"You deserve a medal," the party lady said.

A phone call from the party representative was followed by a ten-minute wait; then there was a knock at the door. A man entered holding a document with a government stamp on it. It had been issued in record time by the marriage court. Chen was a single man. His wife was ecstatic. In fact, she seemed happier at their breakup than she had been on their wedding day – to say nothing of their wedding night.

So, Chen was pleased when only six weeks later word had come that he was wanted in Shanghai. For once timing had worked in his favour. And then there was Lily. If Chen were honest with himself he'd admit that what little energy he had for patching up his marriage had dissipated after he'd met Lily. He found her infinitely appealing – although totally out of his league.

Chen turned the titanium cage over. He was good with tools and understood technological things with surprising ease. He admired the skilled welding joins for a moment and then held the cage at arm's-length. His keen eye immediately saw the complex internal symmetries of the piece. This was not a craftsman's work but rather that of an artist.

Artwork executed in metal was a rarity in China. Painting was common, even in the interior of slender-necked glass bottles. So was porcelain and other forms of pottery, but sculpture was almost exclusively confined to ivory carving. Yet here before him was a work of art rendered in the most complicated of metals – titanium.

"Shanghai went through the Great Leap Forward in the fifties, didn't it?" Chen asked.

"Yeah, Shanghai's part of China despite what Beijing likes to say," one of the cops replied, wondering where this was leading.

"So there were blast furnaces set up all over the city like in the country?"

"It was before my time, Captain Chen, but yeah, I think there were," the man replied.

Chen nodded. It was before his time too but the Great Leap Forward was an idiocy that had left its mark. The idea had been to catch up to the West's steel production by putting small blast furnaces in almost every commune. Then each commune, or in the city each urban unit, was given a quota of steel ingots they had to produce. The failure to produce the quota resulted in severe punishments for all involved.

One small problem: the geniuses in Beijing never supplied any iron ore from which to smelt steel!

Initially the quotas were met by tossing every conceivable metal object the people owned into the blast furnaces – farm implements, picture frames, cooking utensils, door knobs, etc. This simply resulted in the increase of the quotas, which in turn forced more and more sacrifices from the people. Before the end of the first year there wasn't a wok left in all of China. By the end of two years almost every available piece of wood had been used to fuel the blast furnaces. The result was the denuding of the countryside and this led to massive desertification of valuable farmland. What land escaped the onslaught of the desert often lay fallow since the wooden farm tools used to work the land had been burned to fuel the blast furnaces. And of course farmers who spend their time working backyard blast furnaces don't spend their time in the fields. Famine was the most immediate and ultimately the most profound result of the Great Leap Forward. A famine that gripped the land and was felt throughout the Middle Kingdom. By some estimates as many as sixty million people starved to death as a direct result of the Great Leap Forward.

The final irony, as if idiocy needed irony to make its point, was that over 80 percent of the steel produced was of such poor quality that it was completely unusable. That left a lot of scrap metal around. Artisans quickly learned to work in the metals that were suddenly so readily available – unlike good clay or quality ivory. In the dawning hours of morning, they could be seen by the furnaces trying different mixes of metals in an effort to find workable combinations. Many became quite proficient creating and working with new metals. Chen's father had been one such artisan. That's why Chen knew so much about this. After all, as the saying goes: "A dragon is born to a dragon, a phoenix to a phoenix, and a mouse is born with the ability to make a hole in a wall."

"Can we get a map of Shanghai from the period of the Great Leap Forward showing the exact locations of the blast furnaces?"

"Sure, but . . ."

"Would you mind?" The Shanghai cop was going to question Chen further, then he saw something hard in the man's eyes.

"Will do, sir." The man left.

"Thank you," Chen said, then turned to the other cop. "Get me a list of all registered artists in the Shanghai district. The Great Leap ended in 1958. That's more than forty years ago. I want to find out where all artists who are presently over fifty-five years of age lived during the Great Leap."

"So, they would be . . ."

"Old enough to learn basic metallurgy during the Leap."

"This could take a while."

"Even the longest journey begins with a single step."

"We don't quote Mao much anymore in Shanghai, sir."

"Nor do we in the country but sometimes he was right. Just like a broken clock."

"Sir?"

"Twice a day a broken clock tells the right time."

"Ah." The man smiled at Chen then headed out to compile the list. Chen was pleased. These Shanghai cops weren't half as nasty as he thought they'd be – and they even liked the only joke he knew.

Then he looked at the cage and stopped smiling. There was nothing funny about a baby in a cage.

The door to the Hua Shan Hospital had remained shut for what seemed like hours. No sound. No word from within. Finally the door opened slowly and Wu Fan-zi, still in full bomb protection gear, lumbered out onto the steps. He pulled the suit's heavy headpiece off and let it drop to the ground with a thud. Then, still without saying a word, he re-opened the hospital door and went back inside. When he re-emerged, he was carrying a large plaster fresco, almost five feet tall and a foot across. The lower half of it was still covered in flimsy brown wrap.

Wu Fan-zi raised the thing over his head – looking to Angel Michael like Moses raising the tablets in rage upon seeing the Israelites worshipping the golden calf.

Wu Fan-zi's mouth opened and he shouted in fury, "What idiot had this delivered to the reception desk?"

Fong felt Lily's hand slip from his. He looked toward her but she was running up the steps yelling at Wu Fan-zi to be careful with that – that it was an antique.

As she grabbed the fresco from Wu Fan-zi the wrapping came loose and exposed the entirety of the piece.

Angel Michael gasped. The exposed section revealed a

beautifully rendered figure of Prometheus, the god who had stolen fire from the other gods and given it to man.

What little doubt Angel Michael had about his mission vanished. He whispered a prayer of thanks for this sign – this reassurance – and faded back into the crowd – so pleased with himself that he didn't notice the round-bellied white man with the camcorder not twenty yards away – or the fact that he'd dropped the note he had in his left hand. As Angel Michael effortlessly moved through the street traffic he thought, "The Hua Shan Hospital's abortion clinic could wait for another day. After all, there were so many other dark places in this town of eighteen million souls."

Fong closed the door to their apartment and before Lily could even put the fresco down Fong was on her, "What's wrong with you? You're a police officer. It's illegal to own something like that. And to have it delivered to the hospital was just plain stupid."

The last word had come out so forcefully that he cringed, but he refused to back down. He was happy that the baby was at his mother-in-law's.

"So!" he demanded.

Lily didn't say anything. She turned from him and looked out the window at the grass courtyard – such a luxury in this city of pavement.

Then the phone rang. Fong grabbed it. He listened for a moment then shouted into the mouthpiece, "What!" The desperation in his voice made Lily turn to him. He was ghostly pale as he hung up the phone.

"What?" Lily asked carefully.

Fong had to steady himself against the bureau.

"What?" Lily asked again but even more quietly.

Fong shook his head trying to clear it, then looked at Lily. He held out his arms to her and she slowly moved toward him.

He held her tight. Very tight.

"What was that, Fong?" she asked, a tremble in her voice.

"It was the hospital."

"The Hua Shan Hospital?"

"Yes."

"A bomb, Fong?"

"No."

Lily relaxed a little, slumping against him.

"Another cage . . . with a fetus." Lily stifled a cry. "In the third abortion surgery. Directly below your office."

"But no bomb?"

"No bomb."

"Why?"

"I don't know. Maybe the commotion caused by your fresco arriving scared him off."

Lily pulled away a bit. "Maybe it did?"

"Maybe . . ." Fong said, "it did." Fong turned to go.

"Do you need me at the hospital?"

"Soon."

"See if the head nurse from the People's Twenty-Second Hospital was seen, Fong."

"Good point, Lily. Very good point. . . . Lily?" He hesitated.

"What Fong?"

"I'd hang the fresco on the other side of the window so the figure is turned toward the centre of the room, not the side. It's exquisite, Lily. Really special."

He smiled.

She smiled back.

Then he took a long look at her and wondered what his life would be like without her. "Call Chen. I want him at the hospital."

As Fong approached the Hua Shan Hospital he was once again met by the head of hospital security. The man's mouth opened but Fong put up a hand for him to stop. Something had struck an odd chord in Fong. A very odd chord.

He scanned the steps. Wu Fan-zi had been over there – the head of hospital security had been exactly where he was now – that had spurred Fong's memory – but memory of what?

"What?" he screamed at himself as Chen's car screeched to a halt and the ugly young cop ran up to him.

"Where is it, sir?"

"In one of the operating theatres."

"Near where Lily works?" Chen asked. If Fong hadn't been so preoccupied with his memory he would have noted the obvious terror in Chen's voice. The terror of a man frightened of losing a lover, not of a man in fear of losing a friend.

The head of security ushered Fong and Chen into the third operating room. The surgical team was standing to one side. The security chief stepped forward and pointed to one of the lower cabinets.

Fong and Chen leaned down and there behind stacks of surgical supplies was the cage complete with fetus. Fong pushed aside the supplies and pulled out the cage. On the metal sheathing that was wrapped around the fetus was etched a phrase, in English: THIS BLASPHEMY WILL STOP. THE LIGHT WILL COME.

Fong looked around the room and spotted the window high up on the south wall. "Do the ORs all have windows?"

"One other does, the other four don't."

Fong grunted, then turned to the head of security. "Has the room been swept?"

"The whole area, sir. If there's a bomb here we would have found it. Wu Fan-zi has been summoned."

"Twice in one day, he'll be thrilled." The man nodded and raised his shoulders in a what-can-you-do gesture. Fong turned to the surgical team. "Who found this . . . thing?"

A young nurse stepped forward. Chen waited for Fong to begin his interrogation. When he didn't, Chen took down the basics. While he did, Fong hurried out of the room and ran back to the front steps of the hospital. That's where Chen found him twenty minutes later. Fong was standing at the bottom of the wide set of concrete steps scanning the now almost entirely empty vista in front of him. Chen approached him carefully. Without looking at the younger man Fong said, "Wu Fan-zi was over there, the head of hospital security was right there, Lily was beside me." Fong looked around. "The crowd had gathered there behind the police line . . . the . . . the . . . the man . . . the white man . . . with the video camera had been over there."

After a prolonged silence, Chen prompted, "Sir?"

"Shit," Fong said aloud.

"What, sir?"

"A tourist–" Fong thought for a moment. "An American. White shoes. White belt. Golf shirt. Reading glasses on a silver chain around his neck. Red hair – though all Westerners seem to have red hair. Freckles. A Fujitsu video camera." Fong was moving fast now and shouting orders to the nearby cops, "Find him for me. Start with the local five-star hotels. Set up a command post in the lobby of the Hilton. I want the hotels to know that we mean business."

"Sir, should I continue to track down the cage?" asked Chen.

Fong stopped and looked at his ugly companion. "Take ten men. Tape off the entire area. I want every scrap of anything brought to me. Then you follow the cage, I'll follow the tourist."

Chen handed Fong the notes he'd taken from the OR nurse. "I had her wait for you, sir."

"Thanks."

The young nurse was country-round and her eyes were dark saucers of fear.

Fong sat opposite her in a small office that security had provided. "Would you like some tea?" Fong asked. She shook her head. "Fanta?" Again she shook her head. Her mouth opened and a few remarkably quiet words came out: "I'm afraid I may vomit."

"Why? What have you done?" Fong asked.

Her "nothing" came out with a small quantity of spittle.

Fong knew that vulnerable witnesses were sometimes valuable witnesses. "Fine," Fong said. "Were you close with the head nurse of the abortion clinic at the People's Twenty-Second Hospital?"

"Who?"

"The head nurse of the People's Twenty-Second Hospital."

"Why would I know this person?" she demanded.

"No reason," Fong answered, then changed tack. "Do you like your work here?"

She checked his face for traces of condemnation and seeing none said, "We are helping these women. Most of them are just girls." Fong said nothing. He was waiting for more and it finally came. "Sometimes, though, it's hard. So many. So small. Sometimes so . . ."

Fong prompted with the word, "Lifelike?"

Anger blossomed on the young nurse's face. "How dare you! We are not killers here! We are . . ." but once again she ran out of words.

Fong got the nurse to give him the basic facts about the use of the operating room in which the cage with the fetus had been found. It had been closed down at 10 p.m. the previous night like all the ORs. But in the morning they hadn't opened up the room because there had been a bad smell that they couldn't locate. So they'd ordered in a cleaning crew and doubled up the use of the other ORs.

Fong thanked her and went to the hospital's housekeeping office. An elderly man showed him the charts for cleaning rotation. As Fong leafed through the papers the man said, "It's almost impossible to keep people at this kind of work now that the government doesn't force people to do what needs doing."

"That so?" Fong asked looking up from the paperwork.

"It's so. This past week I've had six new faces and already I've lost three. Nobody wants to clean up anymore. Why don't you tell me what you're looking for?"

"Who was supposed to clean the OR?–"

"The one with the thing in it?"

"Yeah, that one."

The old man flicked over a page and came up with a name.

"Is he new?" Fong asked.

"No. Been with us almost two months. A veteran."

"What does he look like?" asked Fong.

"A peasant. What do peasants look like – mud that got up and walked."

"Young, old, male, female, what?"

"Youngish. Male."

"Where is he now?" The man gave him a blank stare. Fong snapped open his cell phone, "Surround the hospital. No one is to go in or out." Then he turned to the elderly man, "Find that man, now!"

CHAPTER TEN

AND IN ANOTHER PART OF AMERICA

arry arrived at his suburban Connecticut home the second night after the meeting in Virginia and fell to his knees in the darkened front hall. He hadn't slept since the meeting and its startling news about Angel Michael's activities in Shanghai. Already newspapers were full of lurid stories. A massive right-to-life campaign swung into action supporting the Shanghai bombings with startling figures on the rate of abortion in China. These figures were immediately rebuked by pro-choice advocates. Abortion was back on the front page – just as the old man who Matthew called his father wanted at this time of a crucial Congressional election.

That first night Larry's wife had suggested they pray. He had done his best but he was unable to clear his head of the images that had taken root there. A woman on a table – a fetus in a cage beneath. Larry had no doubt that abortion was murder and that it was the most open manifestation of the wrong turn that society had taken. That it must be stopped before it ushered in the devil himself.

And Larry knew of the devil and his awful works. Until the meeting two nights ago in Virginia he was certain that his profoundly retarded CP-wracked daughter in the next room was the devil's price for his momentary lapse into faithlessness. But since the meeting he was less sure of that – of anything. He caught an image of himself in the hall mirror. His classical "Yalie" looks were deserting him. Yalie looks he thought appropriate for a Yale man to have – even faded or fading Yalie looks.

He opened the door to his daughter's room. For a moment he questioned why he hadn't climbed the stairs to see his wife. Then he put aside the question. He knew why he was going into his daughter's room. She lay on her side, twisted, so her body faced the wall. Her head craned back toward the door as he entered. Her eyes, as always, were open and full of pain. Didn't she ever sleep? Didn't she ever get relief?

Larry whispered a prayer for forgiveness – but not to God – to her. Then he knelt by her bed and recited his prayers. But for the first time since his relapse he wondered if there really was anyone up there to hear him – or if He was there, if He cared. His daughter's hand touched his face. He looked up into her dark eyes and searched for a message – anything that said her life was worth the price of her pain.

Then he thought back to his wild days as a student at Yale. To a beach house in West Haven – and a roommate, Joel, who had become an FBI agent. Yes, Yale produced more CIA guys, but it also produced its share of high-ranking FBI agents. He hadn't seen his roommate for years, but Joel was his class rep so he communicated periodically by group e-mail.

Larry's daughter rolled over and let out a cry. Her back arched in a vain effort to move away from one of her many sources of pain.

"Like a woman on a surgery table," he thought. Then he wondered why that thought had come to him. Then he wondered if he should call his roommate – and tell him what? That I'm part of an international conspiracy? No – that this blasphemy must stop!

Yes. This blasphemy must stop. Of that he was sure. The only problem was which blasphemy. Of that Larry was unsure.

His wife found him the next morning asleep in the chair beside their daughter's bed. The girl's sheets and blankets were wet; her face was constricted in yet another spasm of pain. As she watched her daughter's features contort she thought for the thousandth time, "I should never have let Larry talk me out of having the abortion." Then she apologized to whatever powers could hear her secret thoughts.

Larry's e-mail note to his college roommate was a botched attempt at circumspection. Not exactly an I-have-a-friend-who letter – but close.

In his austere office in the FBI building, Joel dredged up an impression of his ex-roommate before he proceeded. If even a small fraction of what Larry implied in his e-mail was true, Joel knew he could be in the centre of an immensely complicated international incident. There were just too many people in the Washington office who salivated every time something awful happened to the Chinese. And among those salivating were many who were both powerful and very, very pro-life.

So Joel carefully deleted Larry's "what-if" e-mail, then its backup, then any history link, checked for cookies, then applied the deep erase available to him as a ranking FBI official. He thought of it as a cleanser. In fact, that's exactly how it's marketed on hundreds of porn sites on the Net – Boy Are You In Trouble, Pal – But Buy This Cleanser and She'll Never Know What You're Up To!!!

And he forgot about it.

Forgot about it until four days later – when he picked up his morning copy of the *Washington Post*.

CHAPTER ELEVEN

THE HONG KONG SPECIALIST

At first, Shanghai's five-star hotels ignored the police request to check their guests against the following description: Caucasian male, thirty-five to fifty, overweight, six-foot-one or -two, white belt, white shoes, golf shirt, glasses on a silver chain around his neck, video camcorder. Then they heard about the police command post set up dead in the centre of the Hilton's lobby. In an effort to keep Shanghai cops out of their own lobbies the luxury hotels started diligently to compare the police description to the appearance of their hotel guests. Soon data began to flow from the hotels to the police.

As it did, Joan Shui, the arson specialist sent by the Hong Kong constabulary, was in a stare-down with an immigration officer at Shanghai's International Airport, Hong Qiao. She'd already shown the man her Hong Kong passport, a copy of the Shanghai police commissioner's faxed request, and her Hong Kong constabulary ID. As far as she was concerned, it was enough – fuck, it was more than enough.

Her opinion on this matter was not shared by the hard-faced immigration officer across the table from her. For the third time he asked about her exact origins. For the third time she asked him why he needed to know that information and demanded to see his superior. He refused and allowed his eyes to linger just long enough on the triangle of skin exposed by the undone top button of her blouse so that Joan almost winced. "Funny," she thought, "stuff like that never used to bother me."

"I'm a cop. I've been asked to help in a serious case of arson in your city."

"The baby bomber."

She didn't nod. She didn't do anything. To dismiss the fire bombing of an abortion clinic as the work of a "baby bomber" was breathtakingly callous, even for a Chinese male. Before she could help herself she muttered, "Fucking ignorant peasant" – not exactly the most tactful approach to class politics in the People's Republic of China.

The immigration officer leapt to his feet and began screaming at her. His Shanghanese was so loaded with colloquialisms and colourful local idioms that she only got the gist of the rant – imperialist, running dog capitalist, yeah, yeah, yeah, and yeah. God she wished mainlanders would get past this ancient crap.

The man's bellowing brought several guards on the run. The guards didn't bother her, but their drawn Kalashnikovs were another matter. For the briefest moment it occurred to her that should she be shot to death in this situation St. Peter would laugh at her as she approached the pearly gates. "Why didn't you just tell them your father was Chinese and your mother of indeterminate Northern European heritage? And a whore – such things happen."

"My background is my business, St. Peter."

"How quaint of you to think that. But surely you understand that now it is my business too," he said, his voice filled with a warbling laugh.

On second thought she wasn't sure if a woman whose last sexual dalliance was little more than a wispy memory of limousines and champagne cocktails would ever get the chance to hear St. Peter laugh.

Then, without warning, the shouting in the office stopped and the weapons were quickly shouldered. The deep voice of Wu Fan-zi ordered the young soldiers back to their stations. Then his bulky frame filled the door. He reminded Joan of the New Zealand rugby players who played for the All Blacks. Not the fleet runners but the solid men in the scrum. She liked solid men. She instantly liked the man in the doorframe though she didn't even know his name.

When he grabbed her documents from the desk, warned the immigration officer to keep his nose out of police business, and apologized to her for the "inconvenience" – her fondness grew by a full leap if not a bound. Hustling her out of the immigration section he muttered under his breath, "Welcome to Shanghai." She nodded and smiled. And he had a wry sense of humour – what more could a girl ask for? Then he said, "They found a second fetus in a cage."

"No bomb?"

"Not yet."

She stopped smiling. She'd fought to get this assignment because she desperately needed to work on something that had some meaning. She'd had her fill of saving oodles of money for insurance companies that were already richer than some Third World countries. She whispered a silent promise, that this one was different – this one was important.

* * *

The hospital cleaner was coming round. They'd found him unconscious, stuffed into a closet. He had a deep wound on the back of his head. Now he sat, frightened and bleeding, in front of Fong.

"Nothing. You say you saw nothing?"

"Yes, he hit me from behind. Don't believe me? Look at my head."

"Do you know when it was?"

"Before."

"Before what?"

"Before now."

Fong looked at the man's wrist. He had no watch. No doubt he woke with the sun and went to sleep when it got dark. As the head of housekeeping had said, "He's a peasant." Suddenly Fong envied him. "They'll patch up that head of yours now."

The man harrumphed.

Fong left the room and almost bumped into a cleaner's trolley. It looked much like those used by chambermaids in big hotels. The bottom half of the thing was covered by sheets on both sides. Fong pulled back one of the sheets. There was lots of room to put a titanium cage there.

A patient in a chair across the way barked out, "Watchya' lookin' for? You lost your daughter or sumptin'?" Fong looked at the near toothless man. He had no clever retort, not even a snarly comeback. So he turned on his heel and headed out without saying a word.

*   *   *

As Wu Fan-zi drove up the ramp to the newly built Gao Jia Expressway, the Hong Kong specialist perused the new photos of the blast site that he had given her. Then she set them aside and concentrated on the latest facts and figures. It didn't take her long to come to a conclusion. She let out a sigh.

"Yeah," Wu Fan-zi said.

"Your figures are right?" It wasn't really a question.

"Yes, they are." It wasn't really an answer.

"Then it has to be an exotic," she said. "The formula for force has been with us since that British guy ate that apple or whatever it was he did. Even in the matrix of relativity it still basically holds, especially in a confined space."

He turned to her, "I know." Wu Fan-zi slammed his ham of a fist down hard on the car's horn. It blared and a path through the cyclists slowly opened.

"What are bicycles doing here? I thought this was an expressway."

"This is Shanghai. Pavement is pavement here."

Wu Fan-zi drove for a while then asked, "So which exotic?"

She thought about that for a moment then said, "I wonder if it matters."

"How do you mean?"

"I assume all the exotics are available in Shanghai if you have the contacts to find them and the money to buy them."

"True."

"The contacts would be hard to generate but it could be done. But the money involved – I don't know. Exotics are incredibly expensive, not to mention his little trick with the titanium cage."

With a final honk they exited the expressway. A silence followed. Wu Fan-zi guided his car expertly through the thick traffic of Hong Qiao Lu moving toward Ya'nan Lu.

Finally she spoke, "Why not ignore the explosive for now and follow the money? You might get lucky."

Wu Fan-zi almost had an accident as he hurtled the car across three lanes of traffic and screeched it to a halt on the sidewalk. He turned to her, "Explain."

"The force co-efficient tells us that an exotic combustible was used. Right?"

"Right."

"Exotic combustibles are expensive."

"Right."

"Whoever did this wouldn't dare carry either the explosive or tons of cash into the country with them, would they?"

"Not if they were in their right mind."

"Oh, I think there's very little doubt he's in his right mind.

Not our right mind, but his."

"Got that."

"So if he didn't carry the money he'd have to have it transferred to him here – no?"

Wu Fan-zi nodded.

"This is the People's Republic of China, isn't it?"

"Last time I checked."

"Well, the last time I checked the People's Republic of China monitored all bank transfers to and from foreigners. No?"

Wu Fan-zi was too busy calling Fong on his cell phone to answer the beautiful woman's question. When he finished his call he looked at her. "What's your name?"

"Joan Shui."

"You look like an actress."

"I'm not. I'm a cop. May I ask you a question?"

"Sure."

"Are you married, Wu Fan-zi?"

The stolid man blushed. She liked him even more for that.

CHAPTER TWELVE

A VERY LONG NIGHT

The lobby of the Shanghai Hilton was awash with cops and hoteliers trying to give their information to those cops. In the midst of the mayhem Fong called in Wu Fan-zi's suggestion to the section of Special Investigations that monitored banking transactions in and out of the Middle Kingdom. They promised to get right on it.

Fong sat back and watched the mounting chaos around him. He knew that nothing would come from the search for the American tourist with the camcorder or from the people looking into the bank transfers until morning. By midnight they should have some basic data. By dawn it could be narrowed down by removing those who weren't in Shanghai on the appropriate days or in the case of the camcorder tourist, those who are of the wrong age. By midmorning they'd probably have a list of fifty tourists who vaguely fit the description and double that having hefty bank transfers during the appropriate time period. Preliminary interviews could start by mid- to late morning. There was nothing much for Fong to do until that time.

The banking information and the tourist with the camcorder were his best leads but they were hardly solid and he knew it. So he trebled the security forces at the sixteen hospitals that provided abortion services for the greater Shanghai area and left the Hilton lobby.

Shanghai was beginning to prepare for the evening. Young couples walked arm-in-arm and stole kisses in the shadows. Some right out in the light. How different they were from him and Fu Tsong when they were young and courting. He got into his car and radioed ahead to the nearest of the hospitals. The captain there reported that he had been supplied with a small corps of troops that he had stationed inside and around the hospital's perimeter. Fong warned him not to talk to reporters. The man acknowledged that he understood. Fong ended his conversation saying, "I want any Caucasian found on the grounds or even near the hospital held for questioning. Is that clear?"

"Totally, sir."

"Good. I'll expect a report in the morning."

"It'll be there. May I ask a question – sir?"

"Go ahead, Captain."

"Do you think he'll try again?"

"No."

"No, you don't think he'll try again or no you don't *think* he'll try again because you know he'll try again?"

Fong allowed a moment of silence then said, "Are you native Shanghanese, Captain?"

"Born and bred."

"Me too, Captain – so you know the answer to your question, don't you?"

"The latter."

"You bet. Keep your eyes open – especially around surgery rooms with windows."

"Yes, sir."

Fong hung up and dialled the second hospital on the list. He went through the same procedure. After contacting the last of the sixteen hospitals he headed home. But even as he parked his car, he knew he wasn't heading toward Lily and Xiao Ming.

He was heading toward his one place of true calm, his only real sanctuary in Shanghai, the decrepit old theatre on the academy's campus that had been his first wife's, Fu Tsong's, favourite place to perform.

While Fong waited for rehearsal to begin he leafed through the newspapers he'd bought outside the academy grounds at the kiosk run by the smiling boy with the bad teeth. Fong had bought papers there for years. Of late he'd noticed a distinct change in the young man. Now the boy called himself an entrepreneur and had raised the price he was charging for the papers. Fong wasn't about to pay any more than was required.

"You not able to read the price printed on the masthead?" Fong asked.

"That's the wholesale price. I'm a retailer," said the boy sticking out his chest with pride. Fong snatched the papers he wanted and barked, "You, my young friend, are a paperboy in a wooden box, not the Shell Oil Company."

Fong opened the first of the papers and was happy not to see any story on the abortion bombing. The Shanghai paper led with a story about nine men killed in a fireworks explosion, not a new disaster in this part of the world. On the sidebar was a story about China's trade with Taiwan in 2001 – US$32 billion. Fong had no way of knowing if that was above or below expectation. He did assume that once you traded that much with Taiwan it could be hard to make them do as you wished. At the bottom of the page there was a surprise, an article about China sending Buddha's finger bone to Taiwan for display.

Fong smoothed out the paper on his knees. Deaths in a fireworks accident, trade issues with Taiwan, and Buddha's finger bone – was it only him who found those things incongruous all on one page.

He put aside the local paper and took the biggest of the Hong Kong dailies. This paper had an even stranger mix. The lead story was about a new design for the black hoods used to hide a suspect's identity while being transported to and from courtrooms. This was accompanied by a large photo of the hood. Below the picture was an article about a man who was arrested for shouting loudly into a policeman's ear. If that was not odd enough, the whole bottom of the front page was filled with a by-lined article about a man who successfully sued an attempted suicide victim for damaging his car in his fall from a six-story building. It was only on the second page that a news story actually appeared. The mainland government had agreed to allow visa-free trips to the Pearl River Delta via Hong Kong.

The Taiwanese paper led with a story about the record number of Taiwanese wanting to study on the mainland, followed by an article chronicling a 20-percent rise in AIDS cases on the island. Then an article about Taiwan's desire to increase trade with Japan and their Premier's desire for a meeting with Jiang Zemin. "Fat chance," Fong thought. But it was a small article at the bottom of the page that drew his full attention. The Taiwanese were bragging about their assistance in obtaining the release of a young American who had been caught smuggling Bibles onto the mainland.

Fong quickly grabbed the local Shanghai paper. The article about Buddha's finger bone and the Taiwanese article about the Bible smuggler were both in the bottom right-hand corner of their respective papers. Fong put them aside and leaned back in his chair. He tried to remember when religious stories began to appear in newspapers. He couldn't recall. When had faith become central to the news? Why was organized superstition now on the front page?

The director of *Othello*, Roger, walked out on the stage and asked for quiet in the house. "*Mei you fa tze* – it's good luck," Fong thought. A Chinese rehearsal room was often as loud as it was smoky. And it was always smoky. When a foreign director asked Chinese actors not to smoke they assumed that he meant don't smoke now. So they'd butt out then light up again within the hour, the half hour – almost immediately. It was pretty much inconceivable to most Chinese actors that there is a way of acting without a cigarette.

Tuan Li entered the stage from prompt side and the house got as quiet as it gets. The Afro-American actor playing Othello quickly joined her. The main set pieces for their bedroom were moved forward.

Fong reached for Fu Tsong's copy of the *Complete Works of Shakespeare*. The actors moved toward the bed. They eyed each other, quite ignoring the director. As Fu Tsong had told him so many times, "No director can help you even half as much as a good acting partner." Tuan Li sat on the bed and suddenly her Othello thrust his great hand directly at her face, stopping a mere inch from her nose. She gasped but held her ground. Then his long fingers encircled her throat as he said:

"Was this fair paper, this most goodly book,
Made to write 'whore' upon? What committed!
Committed! O thou public commoner!
I should make very forges of my cheeks,
That would to cinders burn up modesty,
But I did speak thy deeds."

Tuan Li didn't move her elegant head from her Othello's hand and, as Desdemona, stared straight into his eyes and replied,

"By heaven you do me wrong."

He returned her stare and bellowed:

"Are you not a strumpet?"

releasing her head with so much force that she stumbled back to the bed, almost falling. But she kept her balance and most impressively her composure.

"No. As I am a Christian.
If I preserve this vessel for my lord
From any other foul unlawful touch
Be not to be a strumpet, I am none."

Othello was once again quickly upon her.

"What! Not a whore?"

To which she snapped back:

"No, as I shall be sav'd."

Fong looked down at his text to get the Mandarin translation for the last exchange and noticed Fu Tsong's note: *The Christians have a god that saves them if they are pure. What is there here for us like that? What for me is like being saved for Desdemona?*

Fong read Fu Tsong's note a second time, then a third. How little he had known her. He wondered if she had ever answered her question? Did she think she was going to be saved even as she fell into the pit? Fong had to admit that he didn't even know if she was religious. He looked up. The Afro-American actor was in full flight:

"I cry you mercy then;
I took you for that cunning whore of Venice
That married with Othello. You, mistress,
That have the office opposite to Saint Peter,
And keep the gate of hell."

Fong nodded his head. If they believe in a heaven and being saved they no doubt believe in a hell and being damned. He wasn't sure it was worth the trade and although there was much of Marxist rhetoric that he rejected he didn't dismiss the claim that religion was nothing more than an opiate for the masses. Fong had seen many things that had struck him as wrong – but evil – evil was different and sat in territory that made him extremely uncomfortable. He found it more than uncomfortable – he found it dangerous. Who gets to say what is evil and what is not? Although not a young man himself, he wasn't at all pleased with the idea that sapped-out old men with beards could or should dictate to the rest of the species by playing on every person's innate fear of death. That these old assholes could dictate the rules of behaviour with fairy stories of rewards and punishments struck him as obscene.

He looked at Fu Tsong's markings at the top of the next page of text. It referred back to an earlier line in the play – Act III, Scene III, line 270. Fong turned to the reference Fu Tsong had sited and read Othello's lines aloud:

"I had rather be a toad,
And live upon the vapour of a dungeon
Than keep a corner in the thing I love
For others' uses."

Fong allowed that to seep into him as Fu Tsong had taught him to do. Then he checked another of her citations at the bottom of the page – Act IV, Scene II, line 60 – Othello says:

"Where either I must live or bear no life,
The fountain from the which my current runs
Or else dries up; to be discarded thence!
Or keep it as a cistern for foul toads
To knot and gender in!"

Fong then looked at Fu Tsong's comment beside these lines: This guy really has a thing about toads. Toads "gendering" together. He should have this checked by a specialist and soon.

Fong found his hand touching her words on the page and a profound sadness descended upon him. He had managed to forget that about her. She had been funny. So very funny.

He flipped the page and was confronted with a long section of Fu Tsong's writing that seemed to have no reference to particular lines: We all die. Some are taken by time and care. Others by a murderer's hands. But are we never the cause of our own demise? Even of our own murder? Can life never get so horrid, the pain of living so great – that death is the better way? That the pain of the here and now is greater than any fear of the hereafter.

It is my job as an actress to make the most compelling character that I possibly can within the constraints of keeping away from eccentricity. A character that is lost in the darkness is less compelling than one that sits in the light. Let us grant whatever possible knowledge Desdemona could have and work from that point.

Is it possible that Desdemona is in so much pain that she causes her own death?

Is it possible that her love for Othello is so profound that there is almost none of herself left when she is with him – that it would be better to die than be so consumed by her love for him? Is it possible that Desdemona is as frightened of her love for Othello as I am of my love for Fong?

When he looked up he could hardly see. He knew he was crying but he didn't know when his tears had started. He brushed them aside and was surprised to see Tuan Li standing over him. He didn't know what to do – so he apologized.

"For what?" asked Tuan Li. "You are Fu Tsong's husband, yes?"

He nodded. She held out a handkerchief. He took it and wiped away his tears then went to hand it back but didn't know if that was proper. The scent from the handkerchief was on his face.

"Is that her copy of the play?" she asked tentatively and reached for her handkerchief.

"One of them," he said.

"Did the great Fu Tsong like this play?"

"She did. Very much, although she had many questions about it, but then again she had many questions about all the plays she acted in."

"What troubled her most about Desdemona?"

"The woman's belief in being saved. I don't think she ever found the equivalent in herself to the Christian concept of being saved."

"It is very un-Chinese that idea."

Fong nodded.

"Do you understand it?"

"No," Fong said.

Tuan Li smiled sadly at him and said, "Perhaps that is why you are so alone."

Fong didn't follow that and was about to say so when Tuan Li was called back to the stage.

Fong watched her and her Othello work the entirety of the scene again. This time Tuan Li took volition and defended herself brilliantly against Othello's attack. But Fong noticed Tuan Li doing something that Fu Tsong had often talked about. He recalled Fu Tsong's words: "This is not realism, Fong. That's life. Plays are done in naturalism, that's art. In realism people deflect anything dangerous that comes at them. It becomes the reason why when I attack you, only later do you think, I should have said this to Fu Tsong or that to Fu Tsong. It is because you weren't able to stay present during my completely justifiable attacks on your person. You are a civilian after all dear husband. But I am not. I am an artist and I am paid to stay in present tense. Hence I can never deflect anything. Every awful thing you say to me goes in and hurts. That's how naturalism works. It is the strength of the heart of the actress that allows her to honestly accept the attack, fall, then rise like the phoenix to fight again. Artists exist solely to share their knowledge of the heart – and what an artist does to her heart by forcing it to stay present is as unnatural as what a ballet dancer does to her body."

Fong turned to the stage and there he saw Tuan Li's Desdemona doing precisely what Fu Tsong had told him an artist's job was – accepting the pain of each sledgehammer blow from her Othello, even allowing the possibility that Othello was speaking truths, then falling, then rising to fight again.

Fong wondered where this strength came from. He would have been astounded to hear Tuan Li's answer to that question: "Faith," she would have said, "Faith, dear Fong."

The director stepped forward but before he could open his mouth Tuan Li put a finger to her lips. For the first time in Fong's memory a Chinese rehearsal room went dead quiet.

Tuan Li stared at her Othello and he met her gaze. She was clearly challenging him to find the book upon her features, the pages on which were written the word: Whore. For the barest second Othello faltered beneath the challenge then he turned and spat directly in Tuan Li's face.

The men in the audience leapt to their feet but Tuan Li didn't move. She accepted the insult, fell inside herself, then rose and withdrew a handkerchief from her sleeve.

It was only then that Fong saw that it was not the handkerchief that Othello had demanded that she produce. The rest of the audience saw it too and realized that they had been drawn into a clever trap that allowed the play to ratchet up the tension to yet a higher level.

As so often in the presence of art, Fong felt full but humble. He knew he was not capable of fulfilling an artistic endeavour himself but he was grateful, so grateful that there are those who could lead him through the heart's dark corridors.

The touch of Lily's hand on his shoulder shocked him back to the present. He snuck a peak at his wristwatch. He had been in the theatre for more than three hours. "My cell phone didn't ring," he said.

"I'm not here, Fong, because the office called," Lily said simply.

After a beat Fong asked, "Why are you here, Lily?"

"No, Fong. The question is why are you here and not at home?"

Fong looked at the stage. Iago had just come on from stage right. Othello pecked Tuan Li on the cheek. She openly mouthed "Good luck" in reference to Iago then walked right past the British actor without acknowledging his presence.

Iago approached Othello with his hand extended. "No hard feelings, I hope."

Othello took Iago's hand and held it tight. "Lie better, Gummer. Lie better and don't ever let me catch you lying. 'Cause you know this play isn't about a dumb . . ."

Iago hesitated and finally completed Othello's phrase with the words, " . . . person whose parentage was at one time native to the African continent."

"Yeah, that."

"Well, after all, it's only a paper moon, isn't it?"

"Moon looks damn real to me."

Iago went to speak but no words came out of his mouth.

"What's that all about?" Lily asked.

"Art," Fong replied.

Lily didn't know what to say to that. She shrugged it off and asked again, "What are you doing here, Fong?"

"Watching toads gender each other," he said.

"Fong!"

"Lily," Fong said, turning to her, "I don't know what I'm doing here, but I know I need to be here. I know it."

Lily sat back in her seat surprised by the intensity of his response. Finally she said, "You are married Fong. You are married to me, not to Fu Tsong."

Fong heard the hurt in her voice. She had accepted the pain but had not been able to rise to respond. She had answered while still falling. "I know Lily, I do . . . I just need a little more time."

"To do what?" Lily demanded.

"I don't know, Lily. Honestly, I don't know."

When Fong arrived home two hours later he wasn't surprised to find the bedroom door locked to him. The baby wasn't in her crib. She must have been in the bed with Lily.

Fong stared at the empty crib and then reached in and picked up Xiao Ming's baby blanket.

He was surprised, when he was awakened at 4 a.m. by the sharp ring of his telephone, that he was clutching the baby blanket to his chest.

CHAPTER THIRTEEN

A BODY

ong was expecting a call from either the banking people or the cops looking for the American hotel guest with the camcorder but it was from one of the detectives who had been at the very first meeting. Fong had ordered the man to find the head nurse from the abortion clinic at the People's Twenty-Second Hospital – the one who had left hair and blood but no other remains in the blasted-out surgery. He'd found her – or rather, her body.

Fong stepped past the detective and entered the small sub-basement room. Like so many other Shanghanese, the head nurse of the abortion clinic of the People's Twenty-Second Hospital had lived below ground level. The small room was moldy and felt close. It smelt of things burnt – hair, cotton, something else he couldn't identify. Curtains covered two walls; rugs lay on the floor. "I've got some basics from the house warden," said the young detective handing Fong his notepad. Fong ignored it and approached the body. It lay on its back on the central rug, its arms out, palms up – inside a lightly scorched circle that circumnavigated the body. Fong touched the darkened circle on the carpet. It was cold. Then he saw it – a thin metal thread – phosphorus. He allowed the shiver to go to the base of his spine and spiral there. Phosphorus. Much light but little heat – *he* had been here. Right here.

Fong looked at the rest of the room. No signs of struggle. Nothing even a little out of place or toppled over. He eyed the scorched circle again, then looked back at the body. Light scratches on the cheeks and just one deep cut at the base of the throat. A jagged ugly wound. He pulled a pair of latex gloves from his pocket and picked up her left hand and looked at her nails. They could do scrapings but Fong doubted that there was anything beneath her fingernails. He checked the right hand – the same. He slid his hand under her body – nothing. He put a finger on her chin and pushed gently. The head rocked to one side. The neck clicked. He looked at the scratch marks on either side of her mouth, then he opened her mouth and felt inside. Nothing.

Fong got to his feet, ordered in a CSU team, and then took the detective to one side.

"Good work."

"Thank you, sir."

"Who is assigned to live here?"

"She is, sir."

"What? Didn't you check here first?"

"Certainly, but she wasn't here then and her neighbours said she hadn't been here for a while."

"Then?"

"The house warden knew I wanted to speak to the head nurse so she checked in and found her – like this."

"Why did she check?"

"Someone reported the smell of smoke coming from the room."

"When?"

"Less than an hour ago."

"He's covering his tracks," Fong muttered.

"The bomber, sir?"

"That'd be my guess." Fong looked around. "No struggle

except for those odd scratches on her cheeks. No forced entry. She knew her killer. She let him in." Fong stopped and stepped away from the body and stood very still. "Her head was facing that way, wasn't it?"

"Toward the curtain on that wall, right."

Fong looked at the curtain then pulled it aside. A photograph of an old woman hung on the wall behind the curtain. "Find out if that's her mother."

"Why . . . ?"

"Just do it, Officer." Fong wasn't in any frame of mind to answer questions. As he shoved his way toward the door his cell phone rang. "*Dui,*" he said into the device. He listened for a moment, then on a long line of breath let out a single English word: "When!!!!"

CHAPTER FOURTEEN

AND ONE MORE MAKES TWO

The second blast dwarfed the first. It ripped through the entire fourth floor of the People's Fourteenth Hospital. It was hard to see how many were dead. What was not hard to see was the fear etched deep on the faces of the citizens of Shanghai and the edgy creep of panic rising like a waking dragon shaking off its lethargy and staring, wide-eyed and hungry, at the new day.

Wu Fan-zi ran past Fong into the burning hospital. An attractive Asian woman in Western dress was at his side. Fong ordered a cordon be set up around the hospital, activated the house wardens, and contacted Wu Fan-zi on his cell. "I'll be back in a few hours. I'm leaving crowd control out here to a sergeant. You be careful in there."

"Will do."

"I want to be at your fifty-third birthday."

"Me too."

Fong hung up and took one last look at the gathering crowd – no Caucasians – then headed back to the Hilton. He was tired of being hit. He wanted to hit back.

Angel Michael had been angry. Out of control after the refusal of the head nurse. What should have been a gift, gladly received, became a murder. It enraged him. So much so that his work with the explosive at the People's Fourteenth Hospital had been shoddy.

His pre-queued e-mails would have already reached stateside newspapers. But would they publish them after the false alarm at the Hua Shan Hospital? It was all getting messy. As he stepped into his luxury hotel suite, for the first time he wondered if he could pull it off – if he could bring back the light.

Instantly, Matthew felt a dull pain start in the nape of his neck. He waited helplessly as it moved upward until it sat directly behind his left eye. Then it exploded, obliterating his sight and releasing wave after wave of pain so intense that Matthew fell to the floor in agony. But even as the pain over-whelmed him, Matthew thought, "Why?" A line from an early Manichaean text floated up to his mouth: "I look for the light but I behold the darkness." Yes but why, he demanded. An approaching wave of pain caught his attention then it crashed, releasing its crystalline fury. He was pulled down beneath the surface of the pain. Then he bobbed up to the air. He sensed the next wave gathering. But in the pause, the respite, a face came back to him. That woman at the Hua Shan Hospital. The one he'd seen speaking English to the Chinese man. The one who had bought the fresco that had been mistaken for his bomb – she was the one who had derailed his well-laid plans. A fierce wave of pain swamped him, but as he was dragged along the razor-sharp bottom, he saw the woman's face and began to plot how to make her pay for what she had done to him. For, as Mani has said, "A bringer of the light must destroy those who would keep us all in the pitchy darkness."

Wu Fan-zi knew that fire is a living thing. It consumes oxygen, constantly searches for food to sustain itself, and like all life, is programmed to maintain its existence and propagate. The fire beast inside the People's Fourteenth Hospital was a wild thing trapped within the walls of the fourth floor of the old building.

Joan Shui crouched at Wu Fan-zi's side in the stairwell. The firewall door to the fourth floor, the floor where the abortion surgeries were, was a mere twenty steps up from them and it was the only thing stopping the fire from racing into the stairwell. But the differential of the heat on the corridor side from the relative cool on the stairwell side was exerting tremendous torque pressure on the metal. The door was already buckling. It was getting harder to breathe in the stairwell as the blaze sucked all the oxygen it could to feed its fury. Wu Fan-zi touched the wall. It wasn't hot but it was warmer than it should be. He pointed at the firewall door, "It'll be behind that."

"Crouching," she said.

He looked at her and nodded. "Yeah, crouching."

She nodded back at him.

"You understand," he said simply.

"Yeah, I understand. I've been around fires since my father first brought me along with him to his work."

"And his work was?"

"A fireman, what else?"

He laughed. A slow groan came from the door as one of its hinges was forced from the wall. Smoke slithered beneath the firewall door. "Ready to meet her?" he said.

"Sure, but I always thought of fires as he, not she."

"To each their own." He wrapped a kerchief around his face to cover his mouth. She pulled out a mouth filter from her bag and slipped it on. They looked at each other – only their eyes were visible. She thought he looked solid, like a brick. He thought, "What's a spectacular woman doing here, at my side?" Then they ran up the last set of steps and threw themselves at the firewall door. It flew off its remaining hinges and crashed to the floor without offering any resistance. So much so that their force carried them some five or six yards into the corridor where they stood in a daze before they realized what had happened.

By then the fire had leapt behind them in response to the new source of oxygen from the stairwell. Joan took a step back toward the stairwell and was stunned by the intensity of the heat. She put up her hand to shield her face. Wu Fan-zi seemed immune to the extreme temperature. Overhead a beam creaked. Joan looked up just as it swung free from one side and headed straight for Wu Fan-zi's back. She leapt at him, pushing him out of the way just in time. The beam sent shocks of sparks up the far wall and immediately cut off any possibility of their access to the north side of the building.

Wu Fan-zi took it all in quickly. The stairs would be on fire before they could get back to them. He grabbed her hand and pulled her forward toward the south end of the building, toward the abortion surgeries, toward the source of the fire. The next five minutes were so intense that Joan could only remember the feeling of her hand in his. Her eyes were scalded with the heat and her hair was singed, but his choice to run toward the source of the fire saved their lives. A fire needs motion. Once it has eaten a field it must move on to another. Going to the source of a blaze can lead you to a calm behind the storm. Although Joan knew this, she had never been forced to put theory into practice. It was the single most terrifying thing she had ever done.

When they finally got to the second abortion surgery, they were stunned by what they saw. The whole room was tilted. The blast had been so intense that there was almost nothing left in the room. Kicking aside the remaining timbers of the doorframe, Wu Fan-zi ushered Joan into the scorched room and he immediately began to take in the blast site, noting details, trying to remember everything he saw. While he did so, she was drawn by some force she didn't even begin to understand to the fetus in the cage. He saw her and quickly raced to her side.

"Are you all right?"

She nodded but couldn't take her eyes off the thing in the cage.

"Look at me," he ordered.

She tried but couldn't take her eyes away from the thing – the being in the cage.

"Look at me," he said again but with infinite gentleness this time. Then he reached over and pulled her head toward him. "Puke if you need to but don't faint. I couldn't carry you out of here and I'm not leaving you here." Something cleared in her eyes and the slightest smile creased her lips. "You're on fire," she said pointing to his suit coat.

"Damn!" he said whipping off his jacket and throwing it to the ground. As he stomped out the embers, he swore, "Fucking hell."

"Never been on fire before Wu Fan-zi?" she said with a quiver of hysteria on the fringes of her voice.

"Dozens of times – but my jacket! Do you know how hard it is to find a jacket that fits a guy built like me? Fucking hell."

"Get me out of here and I'll buy you three in Hong Kong. I know just the right tailor."

Wu Fan-zi leaned in toward the cage. "What does the etching on the sheathing say?"

"It doesn't translate well into Mandarin but basically it says NO MORE GAMES. THIS MUST STOP. THE LIGHT MUST COME."

"The light," Wu Fan-zi muttered, ". . . more with the fucking light." He was on his hands and knees searching.

"What are you looking for?"

"Yes!" he said scooping up metal threads from the floor.

"More phosphorus?" she asked.

"Yep."

"And there's the window," she said.

"He likes to watch."

"No. It can't be that. You wouldn't be able to see much of anything out of a window like that – it probably leads to an air-shaft or an interior courtyard. I think the window is just there to assure a good flow of oxygen." She glanced at the titanium banner again. "He likes to bring the light," she said.

"Maybe, but he fucked up this time. Too much something or other. The last time the building didn't burn. This whole place is going to go up. Look at this with me. I don't think there'll be a second chance to go over this crime site."

"That's why we're here, isn't it?"

"It's why I ran into the building, yeah. And you?"

She didn't say. She wasn't sure why she'd run into the building. Then she looked at Wu Fan-zi and she was less "not sure."

"Force centre beneath the operating table," he said.

"Right. Uneven scoring. Much more force to the north side than the south."

"Right. And so much explosive that it destroyed the planch."

"Could be he got bad exotic."

"Why wouldn't he buy it all at once?"

"I don't know. Maybe it was too expensive."

"Maybe."

"It's getting hot, what else?"

"The cage."

"The etching on the metal wrapper."

"The fetus."

She wavered and he steadied her.

The fire whooshed up a wall across the way. "Fuck, back draft." He turned to her. "Ready for another run."

"With you? Sure."

"Hold on and we'll get out of here. If that window leads to a corridor or even an airshaft we have to head in the other direction."

"Through the other abortion surgeries?"

"Yeah."

"Hold on tight." She grasped his hand and he pulled her hard through a flaming hole in the wall. Into a second surgery.

The voyage out was simpler than the one going to the surgery. Going out all they needed to do was avoid the fire beast. As well, since they didn't need to go to a specific destination as they had coming in, they could keep veering away any time they encountered fire. And fire had one significant disadvantage – it liked going up and they were going down.

When they stepped into the cool air outside the back of the hospital, she looked at him. "You've got ash in your hair."

"Yeah, well you've got a little less hair than you had when we went in."

"Then there's your jacket."

"Just an offering to the beast. You'll get me a new one."

She took his arm and squeezed him. "I'll get you two and twenty if you want."

They sat at a stone table in the hospital's back courtyard staring into each other's eyes. "It's just the excitement of the moment, you know," he said.

"Yeah, getting out alive is a bit heady," she responded.

"Your hair's still smoking."

"Really?"

"Yeah, I like it."

"Really?"

"I'm a fireman, after all."

With that she came into his arms. Her elegance and his rock squareness fit together with remarkable ease. Then his cell phone rang.

Fong's charge into the lobby of the Hilton sent ripples of anxiety throughout the great building. His anger dared even the manager to approach him. So he didn't. The cops in the lobby manning the phones were exhausted. No one had slept. The news of the second blast had spread a thick layer of impotence over their fatigue. But Fong didn't care. Things were escalating out of control and he knew it. Only a break in the case could regain them the initiative, put some lead back in their pencils.

"It's not complete, sir," the middle-aged man in charge of the banking investigation said as he pointed to the hundreds of pages of printouts in front of him.

"It'll never be complete, damn it!"

"Well sir, banking no longer sleeps so–"

"Just give me your best guess."

The man reluctantly flipped through the pile to a red ribbon marking a page. "This man. Tator is his name. He had two large sums of money transferred here from overseas. Each a few days before a blast."

Fong grabbed the page with the man's Shanghai hotel address and threw it at two detectives, "I want him in my office in half an hour. And I want him shackled."

The detectives ran out and Fong turned to the team in charge of finding the American tourist with the camcorder.

"Well!" Fong demanded.

"We've got it down to thirty-eight, sir. They all seem to fit the description and every American in Shanghai seems to have a camcorder."

"Pick your top three and keep them in their hotel rooms. I'll see them after I meet this guy Tator."

After the men were sent scurrying to round up the suspects Fong approached the Hilton's front desk. "The manager," he barked.

Quickly, a primly dressed young Caucasian male stepped out of the back office. Fong wondered if he were an Asian if he would have risen so high at such a young age.

"You know who I am?" Fong asked.

"Yes."

"Good. You have a secured line."

The man hesitated so Fong repeated his statement but this time more forcefully. "You have a secured line."

The man nodded and turned. Fong followed him into an oak-panelled office. Oak in Asia! Senseless when there are so many exceptional hardwoods here, but so many Europeans never really see the beauty of Asia. The young man pointed at the phone and left the room.

Fong flipped open a small phonebook he carried in an inner pocket. He had to check for the number. After all, he'd never called the head of Shanghai's Communist Party before.

The party boss took Fong's call without hesitation. Fong didn't really know how to begin so he just spat out the facts of the second firebombing as he knew them. He was only momentarily surprised when the party boss stopped him by asking, "Has there been newspaper coverage – foreign newspaper coverage?"

"I'll check but I would assume that there will be, just as in the first bombing."

"So what is it that you want from me, Traitor Zhong?"

Fong allowed the reference to his previous felony conviction to pass and said, "I want the airport closed and access to Shanghai by all other means curtailed."

Silence greeted his request. Both men knew that granting the request would cost the great city tens of millions of US dollars a day. Finally the party boss asked, "For how long, Traitor Zhong?"

"Until we catch the arsonist, sir."

"No, Traitor Zhong. Three days. You have three days at the end of which time either this maniac is caught or you return to that small village west of the Great Wall – I understand that you made quite an impression on the peasants there." Without so much as a goodbye, the party boss hung up on Fong.

Fong muttered to himself, "If I don't find this guy, you'll join me west of the Wall, oh great party boss man."

The party boss made a call – a single phone call – and all services in and out of the biggest city in Asia began the process of coming to a full stop.

The West always underestimates the degree of control available to the Chinese government and the country's inherent efficiency. Communist China is not the comically inefficient former Soviet Union or the hopelessly ideological Cuba. The huge number of people living on the relatively small amount of arable land had always forced efficiencies on the Chinese. As well, the country had been on a quasi-war footing for years. So preparedness was a given.

The call went to the command centre beneath the new radio tower in the Pudong Industrial District, across the Huangpo River. The call activated a vast civic protocol – and this being China – there was no questioning the order that commanded all who received it to stop and wait exactly where they were until a further countermanding order arrived.

Within the hour all buses stopped and pulled over to the sides of the road on highways all around the perimeter of the city. All aircraft were diverted away from the Shanghai International Airport. No planes left. Trains literally stopped in their tracks. Ships throughout the vast river networks leading to the Shanghai Port Facility simply threw anchors over their sides and waited. On the access roads to the great city all traffic, whether car, bicycle, or foot was stopped and turned back to from whence it came.

In the third hour after the phone call from the party boss not a single person came into or left the eighteen-million-souled entity known as Shanghai. Within six hours of that, because there is little refrigeration in the city, food everywhere began to rot. Within seventy-two hours, the city would begin to go hungry.

But it was the newest parts of the stop protocol that had the greatest effect on Joan Shui as she and Wu Fan-zi retreated to her hotel room. The most recently added section of the protocol closed all long distance phone lines and totally shut down the thirty-four massive servers that handled all Internet and e-mail traffic in and out of the region.

"What does REJECTED FOR PUBLIC SECURITY mean?" asked Joan, holding out the phone for Wu Fan-zi.

He took the phone and listened. "You were calling Hong Kong?"

"Trying to report our new findings."

He punched a local ten-digit number and it rang. He hung up.

"What?" she asked.

"Local calls work." He dialled a Beijing number and quickly got the REJECTED FOR PUBLIC SECURITY message. "Try your computer."

"It's a long distance call to get to my server in Hong Kong."

"My server's local." Wu Fan-zi punched in his access codes on her laptop. "Give me the e-mail address of your office." She did and he typed it in and hit the send button. Instantly his "in" box dinged. He opened the returned message: REJECTED FOR PUBLIC SECURITY.

"Can they do that?"

"Not meaning to be flip, but they just did, Ms. Shui."

"So, Big Brother really is listening over on this side."

"Not listening, rejecting."

She smiled. "So we're sort of isolated."

"Yep, only eighteen million people to play with."

Her smile grew. "That might be enough, if . . ."

"If what, Ms. Shui?"

"If you, Mr. Wu, are one of those eighteen million."

He opened his wallet and withdrew his Shanghai residency permit and let out a deep sigh. "Hey – lucky me – I'm one of the eighteen million."

"No," she corrected him, "I'm the lucky one to be with the one of the eighteen million who is standing — now sitting, right here." Their hands touched. She was tempted to say something smart. He was tempted to ask why him. But neither spoke – although their bodies did a lot of talking in the next hour.

Fong's cell chirped. He spoke into it sharply, "*Dui.*"

"We've picked him up, sir."

"Bring him to my office and officer . . ."

"Sir."

"As I said before, I want him shackled."

Fong sat in his office on the Bund and straightened his Mao jacket. It was a useful thing to wear when interviewing Westerners. It tended to scare the shit out of them.

For a moment Fong allowed himself to remember the pockets he'd sewn into the lining of his jacket when he was in internal exile west of the Wall. Then he stood up and shouted, "*Dui!*"

A young German couple was guided into the room. They stood very close together. He was shackled hand and foot. Fong flipped open their file. "Mr. and . . .?"

"My wife, Mrs. Helen Tator." His English was fine although the accent caught Fong off guard. He totally ignored the shackles that bound him.

Fong allowed a smile to come to his lips.

"What can we do for you, sir?" The man's voice was icy.

"You are in Shanghai on business?"

"Yes, I've been here for two weeks. My wife just arrived yesterday. It's her first time in China. I doubt she'll wish to return."

"Really," Fong said pushing that aside. Fong glanced down at the file in front of him to get the figures right. "You had seventeen-thousand-five-hundred American dollars transferred to your account in Shanghai on Monday of last week Mr. Tator and the funds were removed in twenty-five-hundred-dollar increments." He looked up. "There's only five thousand dollars left." Mrs. Tator was obviously shocked. She went to say something but Mr. Tator shot her a look. Fong watched the body posture of the two change. They were no longer putting on the show of being together.

"She must be quite a woman," Fong said simply.

"Who must be?" asked Mrs. Tator sharply.

Fong smiled – she did speak English. He'd had it up to his eyeballs with being nice to wealthy Western businesspeople who thought they had every right to do whatever they fucking well wanted to in Shanghai. "Why, Mrs. Tator, the woman your husband was paying twenty-five-hundred dollars a night." The moment he said it he was sorry that he'd ventured into this territory. Revenge was never as sweet in actuality as it was in anticipation.

"Why did you do this, Inspector?" Mr. Tator's question was surprisingly simple and honest. Almost the question of a child asking a parent about some misdeed – like leaving Mommy for another woman.

"Because some foreigner is setting off bombs in our hospitals and he must be getting his financing from outside the country," spat back Fong, more angry with his own rash behaviour than with the Tators.

"And you thought I was this person," said Mr. Tator. "Just for the record, Inspector, I have been paying that money to a registered agency of the government of the People's Republic of China in an effort to secure an infant. It is why my wife is here. It is why I am here. It is what the money was used for. We are unable to have a child of our own." He reached into his pocket and produced a series of Interior Ministry receipts and put them one after another in a straight row on the desk in front of Fong. "Do you have any more questions for me, sir? Or have you done with insulting me and my wife?"

Fong waved his hands and the officers unshackled Mr. Tator. Fong started to apologize but the look of pure racial hatred on

Mrs. Tator's face stopped him. Just for an instant he considered doing what he could to stop the adoption. Then he saw Mr. Tator's eyes. They were pleading with him not to.

"Please," he said, "I will be very good to this child. I will." Fong noted Mr. Tator's use of the first person pronoun. "I know my wife, officer. I do." His plea reminded Fong of another case where a man thought he knew his wife. Fong was just a young cop long before he was in Special Investigations. A house warden had called. There had been screaming heard coming from a small room and the door was locked. Fong had broken down the door easily enough but what greeted him was not so easy for him to forget. A child had been impaled against a wall with a kitchen knife through his side. The mother stood beside him covered in blood, her eyes wild. The father stood against the far wall, his sister behind him cowering. When Fong entered, the mother immediately grabbed a cleaver and headed toward him. The husband leapt on his wife's back, tackling her to the ground. Fong took the cleaver from her. Hatred roamed the woman's eyes – and madness, most palpable. The boy was rushed to the hospital and survived. The husband pleaded with Fong to allow him to care for his wife, that she was sick, that he knew his wife – didn't need to be in jail – needed to be looked after. Fong had relented. Three days later the husband was found dead in the alley behind the building.

Fong turned to Mr. Tator. "If anything happens to that baby–"

"It won't."

Fong nodded.

After the Tators were escorted out of his office, Fong sat for some time. He was tired. His fatigue was clearly affecting his judgment. He wanted to lash out but he didn't have a target for his rage. Then the phone on his desk rang and a glimmer of hope danced across his face.

They'd found the white guy with the camcorder.

Robert Cowens, Devil Robert to most of his Chinese associates, stood very still watching the Chinese children. They swarmed around the Caucasian guests just as they had the other times he had visited Shanghai's famous Children's Palace. He looked at the mass of children, then up to the small balcony on the south side of the vast entrance hall in which he stood. It didn't take much imagination to see Silas Darfun's ghost looking down at the assembled Europeans who had come to ogle his Chinese children. Well, why shouldn't old Silas's ghost be here – this place had been his home. After all, it was the very house in which he had adopted and raised his street urchins – and others, if Devil Robert's father was correct. The house was actually a mansion built in the late twenties. It sat on the triangle of land at the crossing of Ya'nan Lu and Nanjing Lu. The property was surrounded by a twelve-foot-high, broken-glass-topped wall of field stone. On the southern wall along the much travelled Nanjing Lu side, a governmental "photo" lesson was on display for the populace. In the ten simple photographs a corrupt official is captured and tried and apologizes to the people of China and is executed. Throughout the city these graphic reminders that your government is watching you are on display. The forty-two-room mansion, sitting gracefully behind the wall, was classic English Victorian – rendered entirely in dark Asian hardwoods. Lofty ceilings and stained glass added an air of cathedral to what was actually a rural British palace design. Needless to say, a rural British palace – complete with extensive gardens – was a complete anomaly in Shanghai's urban crush.

The tour guide's English was better than usual for the People's Republic of China. A lot better than the first guide Robert had when he initially ventured into the castle keep of his enemy.

Robert felt a small hand grab his fingers. Looking down he saw a round-faced five- or six-year-old Han Chinese boy

tugging at him. The boy opened his smiling mouth and shouted: "Well Come t'China!!" Three or four times. Robert finally
replied in Mandarin, "*Shei, sheh.*" The boy's smile grew and he
shouted in Mandarin to his companions, "This stinky one
thinks he speaks Chinese." The others laughed. Then Robert's
little snot pulled hard on his hand and yelled, "Come! Dharma
Club." They surely meant drama club, but it certainly did
sound like Dharma Club. "You come Dharma Club."

Robert and about half of the large group of Caucasians were
"Shanghai'd" up a wide set of steps and shepherded into an
expansive room that had a raised stage at one end. Unlike the
other art rooms that he had seen on previous trips, the
"Dharma" room seemed to be run by the children, not the
teachers – the phrase *inmates not wardens* came to mind. The
first twenty minutes of the children's performance took just
under half of forever. Bad dharma does that.

Robert knew that in the Children's Palace children were
taught in the discipline most appropriate to their talents. Those
with musical skills were trained to play instruments. Those
with physical gifts were trained in dance. Those with drawing
skills were trained to paint. From the dharma performance it
was clear to Robert that when a child had an artistic bent but no
particular skill – or shame – they were guided toward the dharma program.

The dharma performance ended with perhaps the most
unique rendering of the old Broadway hit *Oklahoma* that anyone, anywhere, had ever heard. As it crescendoed toward an
ear-splitting conclusion a Caucasian woman, somewhat older
than Robert, came out from the wings and gestured to the children. They looked at her and ended the song as if someone had
unplugged them. A momentary blessed silence followed but
was quickly shattered when the dharma kids stepped forward
and demanded a standing ovation. Which they got.

Having gotten all they could from this group of stupid foreigners, the children began to disperse. Robert moved toward the Caucasian woman. She was busy shooing the children on their way, no doubt to get the next unsuspecting victims of the Dharma Club. Her features were heavy, Eastern European. Her nose was wide, as if it had been badly broken at one time and never reset properly. Her eyes were light brown but sunken and her hair was a stark grey – unusual in a world where grey hair is dyed, even by men. In fact, it is about the only officially sanctioned vanity in the People's Republic of China, probably because so many leaders of this huge country are at the age when hair dying would be a concern.

Robert approached her.

"Do you teach the children?"

The woman looked up at Robert. Her smile was wide and kind. Something crossed her face. Was it fear? Finally she said in Mandarin, "I am sorry but I only speak the Common Speech." They were almost completely alone in the room now.

"Fine," replied Robert taking a step closer to her. He continued in his patchy Mandarin, "I could use the practice."

She gave no indication that she was surprised he spoke the language but was clearly growing agitated about something.

"My name is Robert Cowens," he said.

She nodded and looked past him, over his shoulder.

Robert quickly glanced at the door that had drawn her eye. It was half open and there was a long shadow of a human figure cast into the room. Was she being watched? He looked back at her. She took a step to get past him but he stepped in her path. A small whimper came from her – like it had from his mother when she was frightened. Like that which had come from his brother as he screamed, "No, Mommy! No Mommy no."

She pushed past him and ran toward the door.

Robert turned to follow but the door burst open and fifty or sixty little dharma bums rushed in shouting in unison, "Well

Come t'China," as they dragged in their latest helpless victims. In the melee Robert lost sight of the woman.

He finally made his way through the crowd and out the door. On the landing he looked in both directions but there was no one there. He ran to the balustrade and leaned over. There, three flights down, the middle-aged white woman was running down the stairs.

"*Rivkah!*" he shouted.

She stopped, just for a moment, then yelled in English, "Go away!" Then she turned and ran with tremendous speed down the remaining steps. Robert did his best to follow her but the place was a maze of rooms and hallways and locked doors. Eventually he gave up and approached the house matron. The young woman's English was good, if starchy-stilted, "You say you saw a Caucasian woman with the students of drama, Mr. Cowens?"

"Yes, that's what I've been saying to you."

"Like yourself, Mr. Cowens, she must have been a visitor to Shanghai's Children's Palace."

"No. She works here."

"No. This cannot be. Only Chinese work here, Mr. Cowens."

He suddenly realized that she kept repeating his name so that she would remember it. She no doubt reported to some police agency. He turned and walked away from her. Over his shoulder he heard her voice. This time it was confident and proud. "China is a country of great mystery – do be careful – Mr. Cowens."

She watched his back as he retreated. This time it was a Caucasian woman. Last time he'd ranted about some white child. Before that he made a fuss about Old Silas buying children or some such nonsense. Crazy Long Noses were to be reported. She hadn't bothered the other times, but enough was enough. Now if only she could remember who crazy Long Noses ought to be reported to.

The camcorder man stood in his five-star hotel suite with his plump wife to his right and his video camera held tightly beneath his left arm. He was still wearing his white shoes and white belt although Fong assumed the man had changed his golf shirt and pants since last he had seen him.

"We didn't do anything wrong and besides we are American citizens and this is outrageous," said the woman.

For a moment Fong wished he'd worn his Mao jacket.

"We should call the embassy, Cyril," the woman continued.

"Now just settle down and let's hear what the little Commie bastard has to say for himself."

"Cyril! Watch your language."

"He doesn't speak any English, Sadie, look at him over there, he must be waiting for his translator or something."

Fong considered Charlie Chan–style bowing and scraping but decided to pass up the fun stuff. "I'm more than capable of translating for myself, thank you very much. As a courtesy I contacted the hotel with our request."

"Yeah, right – so you did." Cyril coughed into his fleshy fist. "Something about my video camera."

"Exactly. You were on the steps of the Hua Shan Hospital two days ago, weren't you?"

"Where?"

Fong said the name slower, then with the wrong emphasis, then with the wrong pronunciation, finally with the wrong tones. That did it. The man's face lit up.

"Yeah, sure I was. The big place with lots of steps."

"Big place with lots of steps – that's it," Fong thought but he said, "The very place."

"There was a fire there or something right?" said the man with an all too knowing smile on his corpulent lips.

"Yes, there was," Fong said slowly.

"I got some of it on tape. I'll be selling it to the highest bidder. Gonna pay for this whole trip from that one piece of footage.

Everywhere me and the missus go, I take my video camera. Paid for two trips so far and this could well be numero three."

Fong held up a finger and moved to the window. He took out his cellular and called the only person he knew who knew much about American culture – Lily. "Do Americans buy videotapes from each other?"

"No, Fong."

"But this guy says he's going to sell the videotape to someone."

"The news networks probably."

"What? The news networks buy amateur videotapes?"

"Think Grassy Knoll, Fong – it was worth tons of dollars."

Fong had no idea what a grassy knoll was or why it would be worth money. He glanced over. The guy was getting nervous.

"Thanks, Lily," he said and hung up. Then he turned back to the American couple.

"You took pictures of the crowd outside the Hua Shan Hospital. Right?"

"Right I sure as shootin' did, every little ol' face is right in here," he said tapping the camera at his side.

"These pictures are of no value to anyone."

"Not true, little man. Definito not true." The man stepped aside to reveal a table strewn with newspapers from all over America. They featured stories about the bombing of the first abortion clinic. The papers must have cost the man a small fortune to buy in Shanghai. Fong didn't even know that the *Cleveland Plain Dealer* could be bought here. He wondered what they plain dealt in Cleveland. Then he wondered what plain dealing was. Then he wondered what Cleveland was.

"Yep, and just imagine what CNN will pay for it."

Fong took a breath. The pure, unadulterated, unapologetic greed of capitalists sometimes took his breath away. "I can confiscate that camera, sir."

"I told you, Cyril, this is a Communist technocracy. They can do what they want. Call the embassy now."

"No need." Fong crossed to the door and opened it. A slender grey-suited Caucasian male stood there. Everything about him said State Department. He introduced himself as the head of the US consulate in Shanghai.

"We'll make a copy of your tape folks and you can keep the original. Inspector Zhong only wants to look at it." Several men entered with a second video camera and a set of cables. Cyril gave over the camera and the technicians quickly began to make a copy.

"Okay, I guess, but I want your copy destroyed as soon as you're finished using it. I don't want a second Zabruter tape floating around. That poor fella had the devil's own time getting his due."

After the technician finished making the dub he gave it to Fong who took it and headed toward the door. At the door he stopped and turned to Cyril. "Were there any other Caucasians in the crowd outside the hospital?"

"Caucasians? Oh, you mean whites?"

"Yes, I guess I do. Were there any whites besides yourself and your wife outside the hospital?"

"No. Just a sea-full of Chinamen – and women – Chinawomen, well Chinapeople, I mean."

*   *   *

Waiting for the elevator, Fong thanked the consular man for his help.

"No problem. We want this arson at the abortion clinics stopped as much as you do."

"Are you sure about that?"

"Yes, Inspector Zhong, I'm sure about that. America is a big country. We do not all wear white shoes and vinyl belts."

"No, I know you don't."

The embassy man looked at Fong. "Something else you want from me, Inspector Zhong?"

Fong wanted to ask about Amanda Pitman with whom he'd spent five days and nights in Shanghai almost seven years ago. She'd written a book that had a lot to do with his release from Ti Lan Chou Prison. But asking would reveal his past to this tall white man. "No, nothing," Fong said.

The man nodded his head once then scratched his chin. "Couldn't be about that lady writer, could it?"

Fong was shocked that he knew. But then of course the Americans would have known. They had been part of it, after all. The two men stood in the hotel corridor waiting for the elevator. The door opened and they stepped in. As soon as the elevator began to move, the consular official pulled the auto stop button on the panel. Fong looked at him.

"The American anti-abortion movement must be seen in context," said the American consular official.

"Why is it, do you think," asked Fong, "that American misdeeds must be seen in context while what you perceive as Chinese misdeeds must be seen as absolute wrongs? Evils, even?"

The American consular man acknowledged the asymmetry with a lift of his hands and a nod of his head. Both men knew that those with the most guns wrote the rules of engagement.

Fong shook his head. "So in what context should I understand the American anti-abortion movement?"

"Contexts, not context."

"Fine, contexts – in what contexts should I understand the American anti-abortion movement?"

"First as a manifestation of the fourth great religious revival in America. This one is led by Evangelical Christians and sits on several tenets: all life is sacred from the moment of conception; everyone must take Jesus as their own personal savior if they are to be saved; and life without faith is like a beautiful pen without any ink."

Fong looked hard at the man. Could he really believe this last bit of drivel? Fong was tempted to toss the man a lead pencil and suggest there was really no need for ink or pens, no matter how elegant they might be. But he didn't. He'd dealt with Americans before and found them whimsical on several levels.

"The second context," the man continued, "that ultimately supports the first is not religious at all."

"Well, we can both be thankful for that surely."

The man shook his head. "I doubt that. The second context is terribly pragmatic and very political."

"Great," Fong thought. "That's what we need, politics on top of superstition – the great soup of confusion."

The man took a breath then said, "We have a serious problem in America." He paused, evidently hoping that Fong would ask him what that problem was. Fong chose not to be helpful and kept his mouth shut. Finally the man gave up waiting for Fong's prompt and said, "We have way too many children giving birth to children. Both the child mother and the child itself often quickly become wards of the state. At first the numbers were small but by the middle eighties the statistics became frightening. All our efforts to promote abstinence, to offer free birth control and yes, free abortion, did not stem the tide of kids giving birth to kids. It also became very clear that the children of children also tended to give birth to kids while still being children themselves. The inevitability of exponential math was about to break the bank – then along comes the religious right with its message of salvation to young women if they keep their knees tight together. And, it worked. Everything else, all rational pleas had failed but the terror of hell stemmed the tide." He smiled sheepishly and raised his hands then added, "And as you well know the American government backs winners."

Fong stared at the man. "Are you telling me that the bombings in my city are backed by the American government?"

"Not directly, no."

"But indirectly?"

"There are large sums of money sent to support evangelical movements – yes – and some of that money could have been used in these bombings." He paused then said, "I'm sorry. The American government is sorry . . ."

". . . and no doubt the American people themselves."

The consular man looked at Fong but was unable to discern if Fong was being sarcastic. "We've found the cell the bomber works for."

"Where?"

"In Virginia."

"So, who is this man?"

"He's referred to as Angel Michael in his chat room contacts."

"Yes, but who is he?"

"We don't know."

"Do you have any . . .?"

"Nothing. No picture, no passport number – nothing."

"What does the name mean – Angel Michael?" Fong asked.

"It's a biblical reference."

"Everything with you people comes from that most questionable of books."

The consular man let the slight pass. "When Adam and Eve were kicked out of the Garden of Eden, Angel Michael was placed at the entrance with a flaming sword to prevent them from coming back. He is closest to the Greek deity Prometheus who stole fire from the gods . . ."

". . . and brought it to man."

"Yes."

"So have you arrested the group in Virginia?"

"No."

"Why not – no, let me guess – it's political?"

The consular man nodded then said, "Not something you, as a Chinese official, wouldn't understand."

Fong turned to the man ready to fight but the man was taking out a piece of paper from his briefcase and handing it to Fong. "A man named Larry Allen reported the group's activities to us at the consul in Shanghai. He also told us of the last contact they had with Angel Michael before you closed down the Shanghai servers. Here it is."

Fong looked at the document: *"One more should bring the light to this dark place. One more could release the light. Just one more and the light will be free at last."*

"Is this some sort of evangelical talk?"

"Our experts say no. This Larry Allen confirmed that his group is at a loss as to what this means."

"What do your experts say?"

The consular man took a deep breath then said, "They think it's Manichaean."

"What?" he said, but his mind wandered back to his conversation with the bishop of Shanghai.

"Manichaean. It's a famous heretical sect of Christianity that the Catholic Church has tried to stomp out for years."

"And it uses an equilateral crucifix," he thought. But he said, "Where is this Larry Allen now?"

"We don't know. He disappeared with his daughter the day before yesterday. Right after he contacted our consulate here."

"Great."

"We're trying to find them."

"Are you really?" said Fong as he pushed in the auto stop button and the elevator continued downward.

Twenty minutes later, Fong, Captain Chen, Lily, and Wu Fan-zi were back in Fong's office watching the amateur video. Chen slowed down the image every time the camera panned the crowd.

"He has to be there," Fong said leaning for support against the large plate-glass window that overlooked the Bund promenade.

"Go back again, Chen," said Fong. "There has to be a Caucasian in the crowd."

They went over and over it, but every face, no matter how blown up or zoomed in on, was clearly Asian.

Fong began to pace. "There was phosphorus at the second blast site wasn't there, Wu Fan-zi?"

"Yeah."

"Anything else important?"

"Hard to tell. But basically it was the same as the first. A cage. A fetus. This time the warning said *"Zai yi ci bao zha jiang gie zhe ge hei an de di fang dai lai guang ming, zai yi ci bao zha jiang shi fang guang ming zhi yao zai lai yi ci bao zha, guang ming jiang zui zhong de dao shi fang."* Fong sat at his desk, his head in his hands. Wu Fan-zi continued, "But no other real leads to follow. If there were more clues at the site we didn't see them before the fire forced us out and that section of the building collapsed."

"Great," said Fong. Then without lifting his head he shouted, "Run the tape again, Chen. But slower this time. He has to be there. He has to."

Halfway through Chen stopped the video. "What about the guy with the camera, himself?"

"Thought about it, Chen. He arrived by JAL six hours after the bombing at the People's Twenty-Second Hospital."

"Sorry."

"Don't be sorry, Chen. It's good thinking. But now help me find a fucking white guy in that crowd of people outside the hospital."

"Are you sure he was there?"

"Yes."

"How can you be . . .?"

"Because this turned up in the sector search outside the hospital that Chen conducted," said Fong placing a transparent evidence bag on the table. Through the plastic everyone could see the note that Angel Michael had dropped.

"What does it say, Fong?"

"THIS BLASPHEMY MUST STOP. THE LIGHT WILL COME," said Fong.

Wu Fan-zi muttered, "Same fucking words we found etched in the sheathing."

Fong nodded. "Play the tape again, Chen, he has to be there."

But no matter how slowly Chen went – the faces stayed Asian.

"Asians," said Fong standing and moving toward the plate-glass window. The new Pudong Industrial District shone hard and bright across the Huangpo River. "All Asians. But he's an American. All Asians. No Caucasians and how would a Caucasian get in and out of the hospitals without drawing attention to himself anyway?"

"He could have Chinese working for him," Lily answered.

Fong touched the glass. "No he couldn't," Fong thought. He caught his reflection in the window. He was beginning to look like an old man. Maybe it was just the exhaustion. Or maybe it was the fear that he was nowhere with this case. "And this guy's going to strike again – and soon," he whispered to the window. *"One more should bring the light to this dark place. One more could release the light. Just one more and the light will be free at last."*

"Fong?" Lily prompted.

Suddenly Fong lashed out at his image in the plate-glass window. The thick pane shattered from the impact of his fist. Lily shrieked. Wu Fan-zi ran to his old friend but Fong pushed him aside. "Don't you all understand! We have a mad man on the streets of our city and we have nothing – not a single fucking clue who he is."

CHAPTER FIFTEEN

DEVIL ROBERT TWO

obert peeled off another 1,000-yuan note and put it on the dirty tablecloth. Across from him the small man eyed the money with the kind of disdain that Robert had come to expect. On the far side of the restaurant, an aging beauty was showing a new girl how to properly deliver a drink to a table. Much attention was given to turning the body so that the customer would be looking directly at the young waitress's chest.

Why did his informants always want to meet in cheesy places like this? Well, better than the new "high concept" restaurants that were all the thing in Shanghai. The newest and most successful of these was an eatery called Cool Chains that was a mock-up of a Chinese federal prison. Diners ate in their own cells, receiving their food through a metal slot. Ridiculous.

The man across the table cleared his throat. "Go ahead, spit. It doesn't bother me," Robert thought.

At first, bribing people for information about the fate of his sister Rivkah had been difficult for him. But over his three years of inquiry he had acquired an appreciation for the finer points of the art. In fact, he had of late, gained a genuine taste for it. Just as he had for the gelatinous Shanghanese dishes that made most Westerners' gorges rise.

The man across the table extended a pinky finger with a long buffed nail and poked at the money as if he were not sure whether it was alive or dead. The finger retracted. Robert added another 1,000-yuan note to the pile. The man smiled. Robert had done this little dance many times and knew he was now close to getting answers to his questions.

His investigations had taken him down two paths. The first had to do with the events leading up to and the eventual period of the Jewish ghetto in Shanghai. It was relatively easy to find this information and not all that expensive. But the second path of investigation, into the life of the infamous Iraqi Jew Silas Darfun, had taxed both his ingenuity and the bankroll he had amassed from his illegal trading in antiquities.

Silas Darfun had somehow, even in death, erected tall thick walls around his secrets. Robert hoped the man across the table might just show him a way over those walls.

"And you would like to know what precisely about Mr. Darfun?"

"You were his gardener?"

"One of his gardeners. It was a big place. It needed many gardeners."

"And you were with him during the war?"

The man cocked his head and gave a crooked smile. "And what war is it that you refer to? The war of liberation?"

Robert hadn't met this form of resistance before. The man knew perfectly well which war he was talking about but Robert didn't know the name the Chinese used for the Second World War. While doing work in the American South Robert had been astonished to hear the American Civil War referred to by Southerners as the war between the states or the war of northern aggression. He'd quickly learned that south of the Mason/Dixon line referring to the conflict by anything but those two terms led to an intense silence. So he feared not being able to come up with the Chinese name for WW II would silence this gardener.

"The time of Japanese occupation."

"Yes, I was there throughout that time."

Fine, that hurdle was behind him. "Were you there when Mr. Darfun took in the children?"

The man pulled out a cigarette, a Snake Charmer, and struck a match against the table. Robert controlled his impulse to pull away from the flame. A bitter cloud of smoke escaped the man's lips, then he began to cough. The cough shook him like a strong wind does a piece of laundry satayed out an apartment window on a bamboo pole. The shaking subsided and he picked a tiny brown flake off his tongue as if that bit of tobacco had caused the coughing fit.

"Which children would that be?"

Robert knew that Silas had gained intense notoriety in both Shanghai's Chinese and Jewish communities when he married his Chinese mistress. He had also ruffled many feathers when he and his wife took in forty street children and raised them as their own. Robert looked at the man.

The man smiled thinly and let out another bitter cloud of smoke, "Ah, you don't mean the street children – you mean the Jew brats?" Robert's shocked look seemed to please him. "You have been asking questions about Mr. Darfun for almost three years now. Surely you don't think you have been able to keep such inquiries secret."

He had. In fact he'd never really considered that the Chinese men and women he had bribed for information would even admit to having talked to him. Why should they? He looked at the man. How little he understood these people. Then he smiled. How little they understood him.

Fine.

"Yeah, the Jew brats."

"I was there then."

"Did Silas keep a record of their names?"

"Of course."

Robert waited but the man said nothing. He stared at the 1,000-yuan note. Robert put three more 1,000-yuan notes beside them. The man reached over and folded the bills together, then pocketed them. "Are these the proceeds from sales of the price-less cave frescos, books, and statues from my country's glorious past?"

Again Robert found himself surprised. Odd that a gardener would be so well informed. He put on his best "fuck you" smile and said, "You wouldn't be suggesting that I am involved in smuggling antiquities, would you?"

The man met Robert's fuck-you smile with one of his own. "No – not suggesting – knowing."

"Knowing what?"

"That you are a smuggler, Mr. Robert Cowens."

A smuggler. Not a usual occupation for a nice Jewish boy. But then again Robert wasn't all that nice and he wasn't Jewish in the sense of being religious. In fact, he enjoyed referring to himself as an active and committed agnostic. Despite that, he was definitely a Jew – a card-carrying, yeah-but-is-it-good-for-Jews kind of tribal member.

A smuggler Jew.

He had first come to Asia four years ago when his law firm had insisted that there was big movie business to do in the far east. "Kung fooey films?" he'd asked. But when they showed him the grosses from the latest Jett Li film he'd whistled through the gap in his front teeth. Then they showed him the cheap cost of production. He calculated the net profit without their help. All he asked was, "When's my flight?"

It was that night. He flew to Chicago then transferred planes. The JAL flight took him up the Mackenzie River, over the pole, then down to Hong Kong. He'd lived in Canada all his life but had never even remotely appreciated the vastness of the country until that trip. He didn't even know where Great Slave

Lake was until he saw it slide beneath the belly of the plane. It changed him. But not the way turning forty had changed him or the way leaving his wife had. He had touched the Plexiglas window of the plane and sensed the movement of time through the vibrations. He allowed himself to think about his recently deceased father – and their snooker games.

Robert used to play snooker with his father every Wednesday right up until six weeks before he died. They'd lunch together at his father's golf club – his father still played well into his late eighties. Robert never played. The two of them would eat downstairs at the snack bar, then retreat to the large L-shaped room that was known as the men's section. Truth be told, the women referred to it as the *old* men's section. There were a few card tables, a glassed-in smoking area, a large-screen television usually tuned to a station that had stock quotes running across the bottom, and a single full-sized snooker table.

At the card tables, gin rummy was the game but bullshitting was the entertainment. The elderly Jewish men seated there were the last remnants of their kind. The very end of the European Jews in North America. "From whence we came," Robert thought as he watched an old guy slam his cards down on the table and announce to the room, "I got a hard on for this one." Robert looked back at the pool table where his father was carefully setting up the snooker balls. The man at the card table who had shouted was named Itch. Or at least that's what he was called. Robert assumed he didn't like the nickname. At least it could have been grammatically correct: Itchy. Well, whether that mattered to Itch or whether he did or didn't like the appellation, Robert was certain of one thing about Itch. The man hadn't had a hard on – for a card game or much of anything else – for quite some time.

Robert's father broke the stack of red balls, being careful to hit the cue ball so it travelled back down table. Despite his age,

Robert's father was a good snooker player. For as long as Robert could remember, his father had been a good snooker player. As he walked over to the cue ball, Robert remembered how his father had convinced his crazy mother to allow him to buy a pool table for the basement of their house: "It will keep the boys out of the pool halls."

Robert came down on the very first day the pool table arrived and grabbed a cue. His father took it from him and showed him how to form a bridge with his seven-year-old hand. He wouldn't let Robert even hit a ball until he could glide the pool stick across his bridged fingers perfectly parallel to the green felt surface for a full three feet. That took more than a week of practice.

Robert never forgot the feel of finally hitting cue to ball. The solidity of it pleased him. But it was the pure mathematics of the game – the controlled, totally non-subjective reality of it – that hooked him. His father insisted that he learn how to play English billiards first. He blocked the pockets with plugs and put a red ball and a black ball and a white ball on the table. "The black is yours. The white is mine. The red is common. Now make your ball hit my ball, bounce off a rail, then hit the red. Each time you do, it's worth two points." There were no sinking balls in the game. Just caroms and spins to position your cue ball. Robert lost that first game 100 to 8. After three months of practice, his father finally removed the pocket plugs. He took three red balls and put them in an arc about a foot and a half away from a side pocket. Then he took the cue ball and put it down table on the snooker spot for the pink ball. "When you can pot each of those balls twenty times in a row without a miss, call me." Then he left. It took Robert just under two months to accomplish this task.

Thereafter he and his father played nightly. Snooker. Only snooker. The only night he didn't play with his father was on Thursdays when his father had his cronies over and there was big money changing hands in the basement – sometimes over single shots.

Robert remembered returning home one Thursday night after a summer evening of carousing with his high school friends and hearing his father and his buddies whooping it up downstairs. Maybe it was his desire to show off his skills with a cue stick – or maybe it was the false courage induced by the excellent Lebanese hashish that coursed through his veins – for whatever reason, Robert found himself downstairs – $120 of his hard-earned dollars on the table, a pool cue in his seventeen-year-old hands.

His father took every penny from him in less than an hour, then asked if he wanted to play double or nothing on three balls. Robert agreed. He never got to shoot in the game. As he left the basement, hurt and angry, his father spoke to him. "Two lessons, Robert. One, don't ever make any decisions about money when you're in that 'condition,' and two, you'll pay me back every penny before you spend a single penny on anything else. Is that clear?" Robert nodded. His father patted his cheek hard and said, "Check on your mother before you go to bed. I don't want her wandering the halls."

Robert ignored the order, assuming his father must have been light on his insulin dosage that day. His mother had been dead for some eight years at that point. Robert didn't ignore the rest of the order though, and paid back every penny he owed his father. And $240 was a fortune to a seventeen year old in 1965. But the lesson was worth the cost he thought, as his father's liver-spotted hands began to shake causing his cue to tap a red ball to his left. All those years later, Robert once again worried that his father had forgotten to take his insulin shot.

Snippets of conversations floated over from the card table:

What a cash-business he had.

You bet, you wanted a coat you went to Morty, period.

But not pants.

Nah, never. Morty's pants were fercached.

Pants can't be fercached.

Why not?

'Cause they can't, people yes, God sure, your procrastinate, usually, but not pants.

Why not?

He asks again.

Again I ask.

'Cause pal o' mine, it makes no sense – pants can't be fercached *and that's that.*

Listen to him, the dentist's the expert.

In this yes.

Want to take a peek at a crown in my mouth?

Thanks no, it's your play and I got a hard on for this one.

Why should this hand be different from all other hands?

The rummy player's fir cushes.

Don't start.

An unexpected silence descended on the room. Robert looked up from his shot. He knew what he'd see – someone much nearer to the end than the other elderly men must have entered. Such quiet always greeted the cold breath of near-death.

"Cancer," his father said a little too loud.

The man's clothes hung from his frame like limp things on a line. Robert couldn't place the man's face, but then again, near the end so many looked alike.

"Cancer," his father repeated. "What ball are we on?"

"We're not up to potting the balls in order yet, Dad."

"Yeah, yeah, I know. I meant have I sunk a red ball!"

"Yeah. You can shoot any coloured ball you want."

He hadn't but who cared? Robert watched the slow shamble of the cancer man through the over-air-conditioned room. The man went to the door at the far end and was pulling on it when it needed to be pushed. Robert put down his cue and opened the door for the cancer man. The man smiled at him – the word *rictus* popped into Robert's head. Robert forced a smile to his lips.

"Cancer," his father repeated as Robert returned to the table. He was about to respond when his father added, "I wish that fucking Silas Darfun had had cancer."

Robert's father was proud of being a professional. He was not a merchant and seldom used profanity – but the real new information was the weirdly named Silas Darfun.

"Silas who?" Robert prompted.

"Darfun – Silas Darfun. The Sephardic Jew from Iraq. You know, in Shanghai."

Robert hadn't been born when the family was in Shanghai but he let that pass. Again Robert wondered if his father had forgotten to take his insulin shot.

"In Shanghai?" he prompted again.

"Yeah, Robert, where else but Shanghai?"

Robert's parents had gotten out of Austria in August of 1937 but they'd been refused visas to Australia, the United States, England, Canada, and New Zealand. Only China had granted them an entry visa. They'd made their way overland to the Middle Kingdom where they lived out the war in the relative security of Japanese-controlled Shanghai.

True, his informants had told him that it got tense after Pearl Harbor when the German ambassador arrived with Berlin's plans for the Final Solution for the Jews of Shanghai. In February 1943 an "isolation area for Jews" was set up. In the next three months over a thousand Jewish families were moved from their 811 apartments into a sectioned-off part of the city that was less than two square kilometres. Their apartments and their 307 businesses went to the occupying forces of Japan. Things quickly got bad in the "isolation area." Many people were reduced to begging to live. Some managed to land back-breaking work in the local Chinese mill. Children headed out daily to the markets on Shan Yin Lu or Li Yang Lu hoping to find discarded vegetables and foodstuffs. Things continued to degenerate in the isolation area as 1943 neared its end. But the Germans' extermination plans were resisted by the Japanese who owed much to the Jewish bankers who had financed their successful invasion of Russia in 1904. In fact, the German final solution for Shanghai's Jews never came to pass. The isolation area lasted for 561 days ending with the German defeat by the Allies. Just over three hundred of the ghetto dwellers had died of disease and hunger. But to be fair, Robert's research had also revealed that many people in Shanghai at that time died of the same two maladies.

Robert had found out that it wasn't the deaths that caused so much hurt and anxiety in the Jewish community. It was something, in its own way, far more sinister. It had cost a lot of money, but Robert had bought access to records that showed that seven of the ghettoed Jewish women had applied for and were permitted to become prostitutes servicing the occupying Japanese forces – and at least ten Jewish children had been sold.

One of these children was Robert's mad mother's first-born, Rivkah.

"She sold our first-born, Rivkah," his father said, "to this Silas Darfun. She was pregnant. She needed food to nourish the baby inside her. She had been told that Silas Darfun treated children well and that they would be returned when the war was over. That's what she was led to believe.

"When we were finally released from the ghetto we went to get Rivkah back. We couldn't get past the security guards around the Darfun mansion. Your mother waited day and night for weeks outside that gate to get a chance to talk to the great man."

"It made her the way she was, Robert. Even the birth of you boys only momentarily rescued her. Then back she'd go. It poisoned her. She never trusted anyone ever again. No trust – no love." He raised his arms in the ancient gesture of "What's to do?"

No trust – no love – so simple. So true. So true in Robert's life.

His father had done the best he could to give Robert and his two brothers a caring home, but Robert was aware at a very early age that his mother's volatile temper could erupt at any time. Robert never brought friends home. He often awakened to his mother's screaming accusations at phantoms in the darkened hallways of their house.

"So that's what that was all about," Robert thought. "Why do old Europeans keep so many secrets?" He stepped forward and took the pool cue out of his father's hands.

"Are we finished? There are still balls–"

"No, we're not finished. Did you ever see Rivkah again, Dad?"

"Who knows? Your mother claimed she saw her the day before we were to board the ship to leave Shanghai. A tiny, filthy white girl was asleep in the garbage at the end of a stinking alley. Your mother raced to her, calling her name. The girl bit your mother's hand – drew blood – then ran away. So fast. So very fast. I refused to chase after her. Your mother never never forgave me for that. We boarded the ship the next day."

"And the baby Mom was carrying?"

"Born dead. God's a swell guy, Robbie. A real swell guy. Like fucking Silas Darfun."

"What happened to this Silas Darfun?"

"I don't know. May he rot in hell with fucking cancer."

"You seek the records of those Jew children?"

"I do," said Robert eyeing the man across the table more seriously now than before.

The man stood up and Robert leapt to his feet. "You are a rich man, Mr. Cowens. You may even be a smart man. But you have one great disadvantage in your search."

"And that would be?"

"You are a white man in an Asian country. And the documents you seek are now State property. They are controlled by men of my colour, not yours. I wish you well in your search." He began to move then stopped. "Are you a betting man, Mr. Cowens?"

"Are you?"

He raised his shoulders, almost Yiddisha, and said in answer to Robert's question, "I'm Chinese, so naturally I am a betting man. I asked if you were a betting man?"

"It seems I've become one at this late juncture in my life."

"Well, I'd be careful, because I wouldn't bet a single yuan on your chances of ever tracking down whoever it is you think Old Silas had in his house during what you people so egotistically call the Second World War." The man took a final look at the young waitress-in-training's chest, then left without saying another word to Robert.

Robert had one last contact before he was left with no other option but a frontal assault upon the Chinese bureaucracy: an elderly woman who had been one of the Chinese street urchins saved by the Darfuns in the mid-thirties. Her name had cost him a small fortune and forced him into some hasty and probably ill-advised dealings in the antique markets. Finding her had taken all his wits. When they finally met face-to-face – him kneeling on the wet pavement because she was a seller of five-spiced eggs – he was disappointed by her information.

Sitting on her little bamboo stool, she stirred her pot slowly, allowing the ancient eggs to take in the five secret ingredients that she had added that morning to the boiling water. The smell coming from the pot reminded Robert of something that grew between your toes. He smiled at her. She smiled back. Only a single tooth remained in her mouth. He asked his question.

She took a moment to look at him then responded that she

didn't know the names. "Those Jewish children all looked alike. Now that I am older I can be honest. I can't tell one of you white people from another. It amazes me that you can." She stirred the pot. The toe-cheese smell almost overwhelmed Robert.

Then she added one piece of information that caught Robert completely off guard.

"Only the men," she said.

"I'm sorry, I'm not following you."

"Silas only dealt with the men from the ghetto. He never did business with women. Never."

"But–"

"Never with women. And only with the men when they proved they were in desperate need. Usually because they were sick or something."

"Listen, I think my mother was pregnant and needed food. Could that be a reason that Silas would take a girl into his house?"

"No. He would have taken in the mother."

That shocked Robert. "Did he take in pregnant women?"

"When he could. But there were few pregnant women. Lack of food makes conception difficult."

"What happened to the children he took in?"

"Their parents all came for them at the end. Silas educated the girls. That's why they were there."

"They weren't used by him. Used in his factories or whatever he did?"

She smiled at him sadly. "No. He was a trader, Mr. Cowens. He had no use for young girls."

* * *

Fong allowed his now bloodied hands to touch the large piece of glass that still hung down from the top of the window frame. He saw his image buried in the glass. Him standing in the room looking out; his image, perfect, stuck in the shard of glass looking in.

He watched his image smile.

Then he turned to Lily, "Do you remember the riddle you told me?"

"Yes. You solved it, Fong," answered Lily.

"I did." Fong looked to the men. "Are you good at riddles?" Wu Fan-zi and Chen couldn't have been more surprised if Fong had asked them if they could ballroom dance. Neither man moved.

"Fine," said Fong, "solve the riddle Lily told me. A man and his son are in a terrible car accident. The father is killed instantly but the boy survives and is rushed to the emergency room of a small hospital. He is quickly prepped and raced into an operating room. The surgeon in the room takes one look at the boy and screams, 'This is my son!' Since the boy's father died in the car crash, how could the surgeon also be the boy's father?"

Chen and Wu Fan-zi were both silent.

Fong said, "The surgeon isn't the boy's father. She's the boy's mother."

Wu Fan-zi and Chen each gave a yeah-but-so-what kind of nod.

"But that's not the real riddle, is it?"

"It's not, Fong?" asked Lily.

"No. The real riddle is why is it that people can't solve that simple little riddle. Why is that Lily, do you think?"

"They presuppose that a doctor . . ."

". . . must be male." Fong completed his wife's statement. "Just like we presuppose an American must be white."

Suddenly there was energy in the room. Wu Fan-zi's eyes shone.

"You mean . . .?"

"What if the American we're looking for is Asian – Chinese."

"He could pass as a garbage collector and get the fetuses that he uses."

"He wouldn't have been questioned in our hotel sweeps."

"He could go in and out of hospitals and put nasty notes on receptionists' desks without being noticed."

"And he wouldn't stand out in the video of the crowd outside the Hua Shan Hospital."

Fong picked up the phone. "I want as many of the Hua Shan Hospital workers as you can find to view the VHS tape. Be sure to get the receptionist who found the note. I want them to ID every face on that tape. Got it?" Fong put his hand over the phone and turned to the people in the room. "At the very least we should be able to eliminate some faces – maybe we'll even get lucky. That would be a first in this case." He spoke into the phone again, "Use the biggest auditorium you can find and do it fast. I want a report in two hours." Fong hung up and turned back to the room. "Okay, that's part one but he didn't show up on our money transfer checks either." The others readied themselves. "Check my thinking," Fong began to pace. "We know the bomber is a foreigner – probably an American – perhaps a Chinese-American."

Lily, Wu Fan-zi, and Chen nodded.

"We know that what he does costs big money."

"That first blast could have cost well in excess of ten thousand US dollars," said Wu Fan-zi.

"That's the reason we've been chasing down big bank transfers."

"Maybe he brought the money with him."

"He wouldn't dare, Chen. Knowing what he's going to do he wouldn't chance breaking our currency restrictions. Our bomber must make his money inside China."

A silence followed as each considered this new possibility.

"But how would he make that kind of money in Shanghai?" asked Lily.

"Drugs?" Chen suggested.

"Women," Lily chimed in but gave up on the idea before it was even out of her mouth.

Fong turned toward the shattered window facing the new Pudong Industrial Area across the Huangpo River. "What's hanging on our apartment on the left side of the window, Lily?"

"The fresco . . . He's trading in antiques?"

"Why not? If he bought from locals and sold to tourists the profits could be astounding. And it's not hard to get antiques, is it, Lily?"

"No, Fong, it's not."

"So, we're looking for a Chinese-American who has been dealing in antiques. How hard can he be to find?" asked Lily.

"Very hard if he's smart," said Fong.

"And I think he's smart," added Captain Chen.

Fong whirled quickly, "I want every smuggler in Shanghai rounded up, Chen – all of them – now!"

Six hours after Fong ordered the round-up of smugglers, Robert Cowens was standing on the crowded sidewalk outside of the new apartment block on Hu Qin Road. The building didn't give a hint of what had been demolished in 1985 to make way for it – the Beth Aharon Synagogue. Robert ignored the curious looks he was getting from the Chinese passersby. He was desperate. His three years of searching had led to tantalizing bits and pieces but nothing substantial. Nothing that changes one's life – no proof of the need for revenge.

The Beth Aharon Synagogue was one of the last stray pieces of information that Robert had been able to track down. It had been built by Silas Darfun in 1927. But it was what had been in the synagogue during the war that infuriated Robert. Silas Darfun had paid huge bribes to the Nazis to lift, intact, the famous Mir Yeshiva from Europe. All four hundred Jewish scholars had been moved to Shanghai where they spent the war in Silas's Beth Aharon Synagogue continuing their studies.

It made Darfun a fucking hero. He was no hero. "You can't buy your way into heaven, you old fuck," Robert thought. Then he wondered at himself. He'd never given heaven a second thought before. Maybe Tuan Li was right – there is a time in a man's life for faith. It was exactly at the moment he felt something hard hit him in the base of his spine. He began to call out but his face hit the cement with such force that he momentarily lost consciousness. When he managed to swim back to the present, a young aggressive police officer was cuffing his hands behind his back just as another one yanked him to his feet.

Then a middle-aged cop with delicate features stepped out of a waiting car.

"Are you Robert Cowens?"

Robert was surprised at how good the man's English was. "Yes. Who are you?"

"Detective Zhong Fong, head of Special Investigations, Shanghai District – I believe we have much to talk about."

CHAPTER SIXTEEN

ANGEL MICHAEL TWO

Matthew stands at his floor-to-ceiling hotel room window and allows the sun's rays to pass through his fingers. But now it is just light through fingers. Not like the day in April of his sixth year when the splayed fingers in front of his eyes cut the dazzlingly bright light into dozens of dancing pieces. The light was somehow closer that day than the day before, just as it had been closer the day before that than it had been the day before that.

But all those other times the light came in silence. He drew back into his pillows and buried his head but the light was now inside his six-year-old head. And it talked – whispered – invited – took away the pain from behind his eyes.

It was like the matches. That had really made the man he called his father angry. "You could have burned down the whole house. What were you thinking? Were you thinking? Answer me."

"I wasn't thinking because I was watching the flame. The fire makes me feel . . ."

He hadn't even seen the open-handed slap coming. Only felt the crashing pain and wished the man he called his father were dead. It wasn't the first time he'd had such thoughts. They came most often when the man made him play chess without the chessboard or the pieces. "Think. Concentrate and you can see it all inside your head. Train your mind to be still, to dwell on one task at a time. There's lots of brain space in a little head like yours. Enough space that there is no need for a chessboard or chess pieces to play this simple game."

And there was enough space. And more. Enough space to learn hard-line computer programming before he was nine. To become fluent in Mandarin and Russian before he was thirteen. To be able to accomplish every task that the man he called his father set out for him. And there was still space left for his private investigations – investigations into the light.

Snap and a match ignites off his thumb. And light – and the pain behind his eyes recedes.

Click and a circuit is completed that sets a detonator that ignites the RDX. And light. Much light – and the pain vanishes.

But none of the light was as bright as the light inside his head that first time when it talked to him so soothingly, "Matthew, we have been punished for centuries. They have tried to stamp out the light but they cannot. The famous Augustine tried to demean Faustus but couldn't. Armies have been used and the power of popes, but we still exist. And our writing is still here. The secrets of the faith are in the scrolls that we hid in the great desert along the Silk Road. They will answer all your questions – end your pain. They are waiting for you. In the light – just for you."

The light didn't return the next day. Nor any day for eight years. And the light of matches and even explosives seemed dull and senseless to him – and the pain behind his eyes intensified and sharpened.

Then Matthew walked into his first class in ninth grade English and saw the reading list for the term on the board. *Everyman, Gamma Gurton's Needle, The Wakefield Crucifixion, Othello, Twelfth Night, Dr. Faustus* – Faustus. He almost swooned when he heard the sweet voice in his head after all those years,

"Faustus was in the light, from the light, for the light."

He didn't remember fainting or being revived by the school nurse. But he did remember the hours he spent on the Internet that night following search engines to the source of the name Faustus. The first references were all to the play *Dr. Faustus*. He went to a text site and read the play quickly. Boy, these guys had an axe to grind against this poor dude. Sure he made a deal with the devil but get over it! He read through several critiques of the play and finally came across a strange reference: "name perhaps derived from a leading proponent of the Manichaean heresy, Faustus."

He drew back his fingers from the keys as if they suddenly had teeth.

He sensed that he was at a gateway. The time had moved by so quickly that he was sitting in pitch darkness in the room. He heard a heavy-fisted knock on the door. At least he had taught the man he called his father that much. "Bedtime, soldier. We're going to church early tomorrow morning before school, remember?"

"Right, sir."

Matthew put the filter over the monitor. It cut out almost 65 percent of the light. "Good boy. Say your prayers. I'll see you in the morning."

"Right, sir."

Matthew heard the footsteps moving away from the door and disappearing down the hall. His sense of hearing and smell were acute. Odd that his sense of taste and touch were so dull. To the point that he didn't understand why people were concerned with good restaurants or for that matter why they wanted to touch the skin of Marcia Levinski who always managed to sit beside him in history class. Matthew wasn't interested in touching other people or in other people touching him.

The French teacher had been enough of that.

"You'll have to stay after class, Monsieur Matthew."

"Why, Madame Fastile?"

"Don't be a bad boy, mon petit Matthew."

And he hadn't. She had stared into his eyes and told him the colour of his skin might disgust many but she found it beautiful and what did he think of the colour of her skin?

"It's very white," he said as the vein behind his left eye began to throb.

"Yes it is, Matthew. And beautiful don't you think? You want to touch it don't you, Matthew?"

He'd touched where she showed him to touch. She was teacher. The wetness surprised him. Her sounds made him feel sick. But she had his hand caught there somehow. Then whatever it was ended and her face returned from a faraway place. She released her thigh's grip on his hand and she smiled. He wanted to throw up. He wanted to wash his hand. He wanted the voice in his head to tell him that he hadn't sinned against the light. He wanted the terrible pain behind his eyes to stop.

But none of those things happened. He did his best in the future to stay away from French class. Until he was caught and the man he called his father found out.

"Don't like French, huh?"

"No, sir."

"Stupid language anyway. Don't you agree?"

He didn't. He liked reading Flaubert and Zola, but he was frightened of Madame Fastile and angry with her for her offence against the light. Finally he answered, *"Oui, c'est une langue stupide."*

The man he called his father smiled and told him that he would look after this for him. The next day Matthew was called to the principal's office. The elderly man handed him a new schedule with Latin instead of French. As he took the schedule, the man's old hand accidentally touched his. Matthew felt the same disgust he'd felt when Madame Fastile had put his hand between her thighs.

Thereafter, Matthew did his best not to touch anyone or allow anyone to touch him. That was when he started to climb. He learned how from sites on the Net and from magazines. He'd started with indoor walls in DC and quickly moved to rock faces in the valleys of the Appalachian Mountains. Just him and his rosin bag and his flexible climbing shoes. There wasn't a face, no matter how vertical, that he couldn't negotiate. Climbing was his personal saviour, his only relief – then had come the name Faustus on the blackboard.

"Say your prayers," he said in perfect mockery of the man he called his father. Then he turned to the screen and it occurred to him that what he was doing was a lot like praying. He called up a stronger search engine and punched in "Manichaean Heresy."

The initial offerings were academic treatises. He scanned them quickly. He got the basic facts. A man calling himself Mani, born in 216 AD in Mesopotamia (modern-day Iraq), proclaimed himself a new messenger of Light that heralded the arrival of the one true religion – the Religion of Light. All life was a pitched battle between the light and the dark. The light had created the world but the darkness had come and encased the light. The soul was light encased by the darkness of the body. That's where pain came from – the light tries to free itself from the darkness – but the body encases the light. It causes the pain, like the pain behind his eyes – and the sense of falling. Babies were light itself before they entered the world, then they became small hard cases keeping the light locked in endless darkness.

At the end of the document there was a recitation of the persecutions of the Manichaeans and a reference to original scrolls that had been lost. It was speculated that these scrolls contained the Manichaean secrets for releasing the light and that the scrolls probably travelled east into China with the Manichaeans maybe as early as the ninth century in their desperate effort to avoid increasing persecution from Rome.

Matthew found himself sweating as he read page after page on website after website.

Finally he came upon the phrase, "The Religion of Light is the true, original Christianity."

Something inside him relaxed, as if the final tumbler of a lock had fallen into place and the safe had opened as it had when he was six years old on the day the light first talked to him. From then on he folded his hands and prayed in church to please the man he called his father, but in his head he was on a quest – to free the light.

Several of the web files mentioned original texts. It took some doing but he found what remained of the documents of the Manichaean faith and downloaded then printed them. They made a thick pile. In the dim glow of the computer screen he sat and read the thoughts of Mani – all two hundred pages – in one sitting.

The next morning, after church, he said goodbye to the man he called his father, and rather than taking the bus to his exclusive private school, he headed downtown.

By two that afternoon he had the parts he needed.

By four he set off the first explosive of his life – the light reflected off the even-sided Manichaean cross he'd bought and bounced up to his face. He was ecstatic.

The thudding pain behind his eyes – retreated.

When, years later, the man he called his father broached the possibility of going to the People's Republic of China and becoming an arm of God he had said, "Like Angel Michael with his flaming sword, you can bring an end to the darkness and allow back in God's light." Matthew had heard the rest of the familiar rant about secularism and society's failure to follow the laws of God. He had even agreed with some of it.

"Are you listening to me?" the man Matthew called his father asked.

Matthew had nodded and mentioned casually, "I speak Mandarin."

The man had chuckled and muttered, "And Latin." Matthew nodded although he didn't like the chuckle from the man he called his father. "Why do you think I had you learn Mandarin, Matthew?"

"Not because I'm Asian," Matthew thought, but he said nothing. His mind was racing. The man he called his father was wealthy and could have adopted a baby of any race, but he had chosen a Han Chinese baby. Now Matthew knew why. The man Matthew called his father was a chess player – Matthew was his end game. He was being sent the length of the board to become a king – or an angel. Matthew nodded and thought, "Fine. But you have no idea that I have experienced the light." For a moment Matthew wondered if it would matter to the older man. Then Matthew put it aside. The light was his concern; it was his secret.

The older man laid out the bare facts of the abortion rate needed to keep the single child policy in effect in the People's Republic of China. The figures were new to Matthew but the idea was obvious. As was the man's insistence that there be extensive newspaper coverage of the "acts of revenge" in Shanghai – there was a Congressional election approaching, after all.

Matthew had nodded again, his mind already at work. China – a step closer to the hidden scrolls. All he insisted on was that "I'm to do it alone." The man Matthew called his father thought about that for a moment then agreed. It made sense – the lone gunman.

They quickly discussed logistics, then Matthew disappeared to his room. It only took him thirty minutes to get the data he needed on currency regulations, immigration requirements, and web access from the Middle Kingdom. Then he opened the secret panel in his desk, stared at the book on modern explosives he had secreted there, and wondered how he would get his hands on this sort of thing in Shanghai.

Two days later, Matthew found himself on a flight to Taipei with a list of contacts who could help him get established in Shanghai. He knew of Taiwan's fundamentalist community and decided to use the members as a resource but tell them nothing. They were probably infiltrated by State agents.

He picked the code name Angel Michael, took the permitted amount of currency (just under US$10,000) that he would not have to declare, shook the hand of the man who he called his father, took his two hundred pages of the wisdom of Mani, slipped his equal-sided cross around his neck, and set out for the airport.

That was exactly six months ago – to the day.

CHAPTER SEVENTEEN

IN AMERICA, IN SHANGHAI

oel sat in his Washington office at the FBI building and thought about the e-mail from his old Yale roommate, Larry. It was well past midnight. The silence in the room was only interrupted by the sound of the night-shift data processors down the hall. There were three stacks of newspapers on his desk. The first reported the initial bombing in far-off Shanghai of an abortion clinic, complete with its grotesque photograph and the warning: THIS BLASPHEMY MUST STOP. The second stack of newspapers was from two days later. The stories in these papers were all about information of an imminent second bombing but that no bombing had taken place. The papers, with much self-righteous posturing, had refused to run the photo, which they all agreed this time was grotesque, and all were angered that this may be some kind of a hoax. Then the third stack of papers wrote about a fire in a Shanghai hospital that was reported by their stringers in the city. But there had been no previous e-mail. No cage. No note. No message of any sort.

Joel sat back in his chair. It was all pretty confusing but what was clear was that Shanghai and hence the People's Republic of China were reeling. And that was good as far as Joel was concerned. A China off-balance was a China vulnerable. And no vulnerable nation, no matter how many people it had, could endanger the United States. A weak China was a good China, as far as Joel was concerned.

Joel thought about the e-mail from his Yale buddy, Larry, again. Clearly, there was an arsonist on the loose in ol' Shanghai, probably a religiously inspired arsonist. Joel knew the profile of such individuals quite well.

He turned off the overheads in his office and stared at the lights of the Capitol. How to proceed? Joel felt as if the ball were now in his court. What could he do to force this nutcake into striking again? Joel allowed a smile to come to his lips. If even a little of what he surmised from his former roommate's e-mail was true, Joel thought he knew just how to egg this lunatic on to another effort. He lit a smoke, picked up his phone, and called his contact at the *New York Times*.

* * *

When Angel Michael read the headlines in the *International Herald Tribune* claiming that the bombing in the People's Fourteenth Hospital was nothing more than an industrial accident, rage seethed through him. He tried to breathe it away but found himself almost faint from anger. The paper made the point that there had been no cage, no note, and that much more than the abortion surgeries had been incinerated. It put the entire thing down to bad building codes in the People's Republic of China.

He couldn't believe it. Matthew looked at the people on the streets. There were open signs of fear on almost every face – on the buck-toothed youth who sold apples from the small wooden kiosk at exorbitant prices, on the man who fixed shoes from his sidewalk perch, on the old man on the ratty plastic chair with his feet in slippers, on the hunched-over figures on their bikes, on the traffic cops in their raised booths at intersections, on the men lifting, on the men carrying, on the men bent beneath their labours – even on the newly rich Tokyo-suited businessmen.

The women betrayed their fear differently. They peeked out warily beneath hooded eyes.

Mani had talked about the pervasiveness of fear before the coming of the light. And the light was coming. He, Angel Michael, was bringing it. He mounted the bicycle that he had bought from a street vendor when he first arrived in Shanghai all those months ago and he joined the unbroken stream of cyclists, twelve abreast, on Yan'an Lu. He settled into the pace and moved slowly toward the centre of the procession. He had no particular destination, so he didn't have to be on either end to make a turn. He just rode and felt the wind in his face. It helped him to think.

Things were obviously getting complicated. The hospitals were now guarded and he had planned for this. But it was also evident that the city had been closed down. To check this he had tried to order train tickets to Beijing – no go. He had tried to phone a department store in Nanjing and his call had simply gone dead. Even his computer refused to link him to an outside server. So they had him surrounded. Him and eighteen million other souls. As he pedalled he thought, "I can still complete my mission." At least he thought that until he picked up the note from his explosives supplier at the usual drop location.

It was typically cryptic: "Price has gone up – four times what you paid last time. Times are tough. Tomorrow by the great tower in the Pudong, the usual time. Don't be late. This is our last meeting – ever." Four times what he had paid the last time! He didn't have anywhere near that kind of cash on hand and he only had until the "usual time" tomorrow to raise the money. He had to work quickly or the light would never come to this dark corner of the planet. He knew it was risky to raise that kind of money quickly. It could attract attention. But he had no other choice.

He flipped open the cell phone and made a call even as he pedalled.

Chen delivered the bad news to Fong. "Over eighty percent of the hospital workers have viewed the VHS tape. They were able to identity most but not all of the faces, sir."

"Was the receptionist there?"

"Yes, he was very helpful in identifying hospital workers but he couldn't ID anyone as the man who had left the message on his desk."

"How many left unidentified?" Chen took a deep breath. "Spit it out, damn it," Fong barked.

"Eleven."

"Eleven!"

"Sorry, sir."

"Is there a way of getting photos of the eleven who weren't identified from the VHS tape so we can show them around?"

Chen smiled and withdrew eleven photos from his pocket.

"You are good with technology, aren't you Chen?"

"Yes sir. I find technology very interesting."

"Good." Fong spread out the pictures on his desk. Four were women. Two were elderly men. Even if he arbitrarily left out those six, he was still looking at five faces of a possible serial arsonist. He stared at the faces. They stared back at him.

Matthew stared at the two Tibetans in front of him. He could sense their thinly veiled hatred, racial hatred. He'd had lots of experience with that. "Your hatred's okay," he thought. This is just about business.

They showed him several large sandstone carvings. One was an entire lintel piece. Another was an exquisite freestanding statue. Both were too large for him to lug around Shanghai. He needed something contained – something valuable but small. After much angry gnashing of teeth and colourful expletives, Angel Michael turned on his heel. He was surprised that they didn't stop him. He pulled open the door and a small Tibetan woman stood there smiling. She had an expensive briefcase in her hands. She deftly flicked open the locks. The leather lid opened slowly revealing two antique swolta knives on a velvet cloth. Between them was an immaculately kept Buddhist scroll decorated with images of monks in a farmer's field. Angel Michael pretended indifference but it did not last long. The find was special and both knew it. He tilted his head to one side and named a price. She laughed and quoted one back. He cried. In less than twenty minutes he had in his hands the means to get the rest of the money he needed to bring light to these poor benighted souls. Even as he paid out the last of his yuan notes Angel Michael was thinking ahead – to the buyer. Maybe it was time to meet the famous Devil Robert. Perhaps he was exactly the buyer for three such items.

Matthew had trailed Devil Robert several days ago down to Good Food Street. At first he was shocked to see him in the company of Tuan Li. Then he let it go. Matthew didn't care who was in whose company or what race screwed what race. It was a matter of indifference to Matthew. But he saw the value of having Tuan Li at one's side. After all, who would dare accuse the famous Tuan Li, national treasure of the People's Republic of China, of stealing from the motherland.

He had watched Tuan Li twirl noodles on her chopsticks and feed them to the white man as if he were a child. Well, perhaps he was a child but a very useful child with a very full bank account if even part of the rumours were true about Devil Robert.

Then he stopped himself. Why take the risk of a new buyer? He placed a local call to the Mandarin Guest House. A voice answered in Cantonese. Angel Michael smiled and responded in Cantonese. Within fifty words, a meeting had been arranged and the basics of a deal was agreed upon that would allow

Angel Michael to buy all the explosives he needed to bring back the light.

As Matthew got back on his bicycle, the tendril movements behind his eyes that signalled the onset of pain began. He made himself concentrate on the movement. He knew the pain behind his eyes and the releasing of the light within him were linked. How he didn't know. But he had faith that Mani knew since he had known almost everything else of importance to Matthew. And, perhaps, that knowledge was in the sacred scrolls of the faithful, which had been hidden in the Silk Road deserts in an effort to keep them safe from the attentions of Rome all those years ago.

CHAPTER EIGHTEEN

INTERROGATIONS

Few people in the People's Republic of China could enter Fong's office without being announced. Fewer still could cause Fong to grow cold with both anger and fear. But then again there is only one head of the Communist Party in Shanghai and at that moment he was standing in the doorway of Fong's office and Fong was doing his best not to either strike out or beg.

The man was tall. A Northerner. His Shanghanese was poor. He may well have lived in Shanghai for years but he had never bothered to pick up the local dialect. Typical. For fifty years Beijing had allowed Shanghai to rot. According to Maoist thinking, Shanghai had been infected by its contacts with the West and the Shanghanese were thus not to be trusted. So there were few if any Shanghanese admitted to the high corridors of power.

But Beijing announced its change in attitude toward Shanghai when Chou En-lai pronounced the famous words, "Black cat, white cat, what's the difference." This was taken to mean money from the East, money from the West – money is money. And the race was on. All of a sudden Shanghai's historical contact with the West was an advantage. Overnight, Shanghai was central to Beijing's plans. But they never really trusted Shanghai up there in Beijing so men like the one standing in Fong's doorway were put in positions of power just to be sure those uppity Shanghanese never forgot who really runs the Middle Kingdom.

"Good evening, Traitor Zhong," the man began. His voice was heavy. A worker's voice. His clothes, although of good fabric, hung awkwardly on his thick shoulders and almost non-existent neck. His eyes were coal black. His hands were rough as if they had spent years wielding a pickaxe in a mine, which they may well have done.

Fong nodded and almost said, "To what do I owe the pleasure of your company on this fine evening?" but decided the man probably had no sense of humour. The man strode into Fong's office and placed three American newspapers on Fong's desk. "My people tell me that these papers claim the explosion at the People's Fourteenth Hospital was nothing more than an unfortunate accident."

Fong glanced at the papers. "They're wrong."

The man bristled at Fong's refusal to use his title. "And you know this how, Traitor Zhong?"

"Our head arson investigator was in the building before sections of it collapsed. He saw the cage. He saw the message on the cage."

Still no "sir."

"Your man was in the fire? Perhaps he set the fire?"

"Perhaps he didn't."

The moment of dead air between the two men was filled with challenge.

"I'm going to lift the embargo against the city."

"Don't!"

The man stared at Fong.

"Sir. Please don't, sir! We are making progress. I swear it, sir."

"One more day, Traitor Zhong. One more day and you'd better have results for me." The man was about to leave when he stopped himself and stared at the office. "This is much too fine an office for a traitor."

Fong looked at the man.

"Don't you think, Traitor Zhong?"

The man waited. Slowly Fong nodded. "In case you haven't noticed, your window is broken." The man smiled. "One more day, Traitor Zhong. One more day." Then he turned and left, slamming the door behind him, as if his point needed any further emphasis. Fong took a moment to collect himself then opened the door. Several of his detectives were standing there with their mouths open.

"What? Never seen a party hack before? Come on, we've got work to do. Everyone in place?" They were coming back to Earth. "Everyone in place?" Fong repeated.

"Yes, sir."

"Good. Give me ten minutes then put Mr. Cowens in my office."

Robert was surprised by the spaciousness of Fong's office. He looked out the broken window at the spectacular view of the radio tower, the world's tallest freestanding building, in the Pudong Industrial Region across the Huangpo River. He said the name Huangpo a second time. He liked the sound. The bruise on his face hurt but he did his best to ignore it. Something about all this actually felt right. Or perhaps inevitable.

Somewhere in the dark recesses of his mind he'd always wondered if he'd end up incarcerated. On some level he believed it was his just end – on another level he knew he'd always been, in some sense, behind bars. He looked at the desk. There was a picture of a thin-faced younger woman carrying a newborn child. He'd only had a brief glance at this Detective Zhong but he seemed a bit old to be with this young creature.

Certainly a little long in the tooth to be starting a family. Robert noted the arrangement of the articles on Fong's desk. Not symmetrical but somehow ordered, as if planned – like a Japanese flower arrangement. Then Robert dismissed the thought. This was a Chinese cop. Just one step up from a thug or one down from a party man. He set his face, rolled his shoulders to relieve the tension, and stood very still, waiting.

In a small, empty side office, Fong quickly read through his notes. They had been tracking Mr. Cowens' activities for quite some time. They knew his devil and his deeds but as Fong leafed through the papers for the third time he felt sure that their investigation had missed something. Something important.

Mr. Cowens' salary from his law firm in Toronto was far greater than the money he made buying and selling antiquities. He also didn't demand top dollar for a lot of his finds. Everyone they'd interviewed agreed that he was a tough and extremely knowledgeable negotiator but he never seemed to go for the kill in his trading, as if getting just enough money was the goal – but just enough for what? They knew he was dealing solely in cash but he always seemed to leave Shanghai with his pockets pretty much empty of both yuan and US dollars. He had no bank accounts in Shanghai or the rest of the mainland; he'd been body searched several times leaving the country and they'd found nothing. There were only a few small transactions converting yuan to US dollars on record and almost no bank transfers either to or from overseas. The whole thing just didn't add up. Like a restaurant menu missing a page.

Fong put aside the report on Robert Cowens and opened his folder on Tuan Li. He re-read the famous actress's statement. She was waiting in the adjoining interrogation room, the one the cops called the "Hilton" because it had a couch, a chair that had all four legs, and it was cleaned at least once a year.

Tuan Li rose from the sofa the moment Fong entered the room and the smile on her face said that she was extremely happy to see him. "This is a great pleasure," she said.

"For myself as well, but I'm afraid this is a police matter."

"Ah, am I under suspicion of some dastardly crime?" Her smile was luminous.

"No, but you have been consorting with foreigners."

"Consorting is a complicated word," she replied slowly and sat back down.

"Would you mind telling me what you were doing in the company of Mr. Robert Cowens?"

She thought about the question for a second. She certainly minded but she decided to answer. "I was assessing whether he was worthy of falling in love with."

Fong looked hard at her.

"You heard correctly, Detective Zhong," she said icily.

It hurt him that she used his formal title and she knew it. "And did he live up to your no doubt high standards?"

"No."

"Why?"

"He had no faith."

"What?"

"Faith. He had no faith – no faith, Detective Zhong, no love. May I go now?" She stood. She was taller than him.

Fong stepped aside and she headed toward the door. "My wife would have admired your acting."

"That's not fair, Detective Zhong. You can't insult me then offer me such high praise. It is unwise to use the affections of the departed for personal gain. It should be beneath you. It is no doubt beneath the memory of the great Fu Tsong."

He looked at her. The simple elegance of the line of her momentarily transfixed him. Her words echoed in his head – they were true and he knew it. He said nothing.

She shook her head. "You disappoint me, Detective Zhong."

What could the great Fu Tsong have seen in this man, she wondered – clearly he had no faith either.

After Tuan Li left, Robert Cowens' translator was ushered into the interrogation room. Her round face and French haircut surprised Fong. He glanced down at his data sheet. She had a man's name. He asked her about that.

"My father wanted a boy – he got me."

Fong nodded. That happened. "How long have you worked for Mr. Cowens?"

"Three years now."

"How good is his Mandarin?"

"He thinks it's better than it is."

"They all do, don't they?" She nodded slightly. "Are you present for most of his business dealings?"

"Most but not all."

"He illegally trades in antiquities."

After a slight hesitation she said, "I have confirmed that in my statement."

"You could go to jail for aiding and abetting his illegal activities."

"I could go to jail for other reasons too." She stared straight at him. Not so much a challenge as a weariness of fighting.

"Where does the money go?"

"What money?"

"The money he gets from selling the antiquities?"

"Some goes into the buying of other antiquities that he sells later."

"And the rest?"

She paused and brought a hand up to her face. He noticed that her teeth weren't good and although her clothes were clean and attractive they were excessively modest. Modest to his eyes, he reminded himself. She brushed her hand over the front of her skirt and said, more to her hand, than to Fong, "To government officials at first and later to older men and women."

"What did he want from the government officials?"

"Access to information about Jews in Shanghai during the war."

"He's a Jew?"

She nodded.

"Did he get the information he was after?"

"I believe so. His family was here, in Shanghai, during the Japanese occupation and was forced into the ghetto."

"As were many."

Again she nodded.

"But now he's moved on from greasing government officials to buying information from older men and women, is that right?"

"Yes."

"Which older men and women exactly?"

"Those who had worked for Silas Darfun."

Fong looked at her as if she were mad. "Silas Darfun? The rich Long Nose who raised the orphans and had the Chinese wife?"

She nodded and turned her head to one side. "His house is up by the Hua Shan Hospital. It's now the Children's Palace."

Fong knew that, but it had never had any relevance to him before. He knew that the mansion at Nanjing Lu and Yan'an Lu, now a training centre for artistic children, had originally been owned by a wealthy man with the unlikely name of Silas Darfun.

Fong thanked the translator for her help but as she got up to go he said, "I think it best that you leave your passport here."

She reached into her handbag and placed her passport on his desk.

He was about to apologize and explain that it was just standard procedure then he remembered the smell of burnt bodies and decided to pass up the niceties.

Chen was at the door as the translator left.

"I hope this is good news, Captain Chen. With your face it's hard to tell."

"I've been told that, sir."

"So?"

"We've been able to eliminate two of the five men. They were the husbands of women waiting for their wives to have . . . you know."

"Abortions. It's time that we all learned to say that word without flinching. So who's left?"

Chen put three photos on the desk. Two were of middle-aged hard-faced men. One wore worker's clothes and looked like he had some Uzbek blood in him. The other was well dressed and well groomed. The third man was younger. Much younger. He wore quality but not showy clothing. He carried a briefcase.

"A guess, sir?"

Fong didn't know. It could be any of these guys or for that matter any of thousands, no, hundreds of thousands of others. "What about the unidentified women?"

"Would a woman do this, sir?"

Fong didn't know that either. He thought not. But this blasphemy "stuff" was really beyond his comprehension. He shrugged his shoulders and said, "I can't think about that now."

"Sorry, sir."

"Don't be, Chen. You're a terrific cop." And Fong thought but did not say, "And a very fine man."

Robert turned quickly when Fong entered the office. "Sit," Fong said in English.

Robert didn't for a moment then did. "Who broke your window?"

"I did," Fong answered.

"Why?" Robert said trying to be upbeat.

"Something pissed me off," said Fong matter of factly. "Right now, you piss me off, Mr. Cowens."

"Do I?"

"You do." Fong flipped open a folio. "You have been illegally trading in antiquities in Shanghai for the better part of three years. Why?"

"To make money."

"You make much more money from your law practice in Toronto."

"There's quite a large Chinese population in Toronto."

"Is there?" replied Fong wondering what this had to do with anything.

"The largest in North America – mainly Cantonese, though."

"Is that so?"

"I believe it is."

"Are you finished with this?"

"This?" Robert queried.

"This stupid diversion. Are you finished with this?"

Robert nodded.

"Good. So why do you bother making pennies trading in antiquities in Shanghai when you make a fortune in your law practice?"

Robert smiled.

"Don't smile Mr. Cowens, you are in very serious trouble."

Robert's smile went away but he was strangely not sad or even frightened. "I trade in antiquities to be able to find information about a family member of mine who spent the war in Shanghai?"

Fong nodded.

"My parents and their daughter Rivkah were in the Shanghai ghetto."

Fong signalled him to go on.

"I believe my sister was left behind. I've been trying to find her or information about her. But it costs money. More money than I am allowed to bring into the People's Republic of China so I go 'antiquing' to raise the money I need."

So that was the missing data from Mr. Cowens' file. It linked so many of the pieces together and, more importantly, removed any possibility that Robert might have something to do with the bombings. Of course that conclusion rested on the idea that Robert was telling Fong the truth. Fong would have it checked out but he doubted Robert was lying to him. It was writ large all over the man's face. For a lawyer he was remarkably bad at keeping his feelings under wraps. "And have you found the information you seek?"

Robert allowed his hands to come up into the air and then flutter down. "No."

"Perhaps I can help."

Robert couldn't believe his ears. Then he heard the edge in Fong's voice. "And what do I have to do to gain your help in this matter?"

"You are a lawyer, Mr. Cowens."

"It shows?"

Fong nodded but didn't smile. He made a decision.

Robert spread his arms in submission then repeated his question, "What do I have to do to gain your help in this matter?"

"Help me find the man who is setting bombs in our hospitals."

Robert was astounded by the request. "And how would I do that?"

"We believe he 'antiques' just as you do to raise his capital."

Robert thought about that for a moment then rubbed his chin.

"Did you hurt yourself when you stumbled and fell to the pavement?"

Robert didn't miss the use of the word *stumbled* in "stumbled and fell to the pavement" and realized his acceptance of that version of the story was part of the deal. Naturally – this was China, after all. "Yeah, a bit," he said.

"Believe me, Mr. Cowens, that pain is nothing compared to what I can inflict upon you if you don't help us find this killer."

"That's a very persuasive argument. Not elegant but persuasive."

"I would have thought that helping you find information about your lost sister would have been incentive enough."

"It is."

"Good. I have no love of violence, Mr. Cowens."

"Really! Do you carry a gun?"

"No."

"Why not?"

"I'm an awful shot."

Robert was tempted to laugh but quickly realized that was not such a good idea.
"Okay, give me a hint where to start with this guy. What do you know about the bomber?"

Fong went through the basics of what they knew of Angel Michael. Robert sat impassively listening. Fong finished. Robert didn't move.

"Does that give you a place to start your search?"

Robert thought about it for a full ten seconds then said, "No. I'm sorry, but it doesn't."

Fong swore in Mandarin. Robert got the gist – something about a goat's testicles. He said nothing. He had nothing to say. He did wonder if Fong was pissed off enough to break something else – maybe him.

There was another very long silence in the room then Fong remembered the words of the American consular official and turned to Robert. Robert took a half-step back. "He's a Manichaean apparently."

"A what?"

"A Manichaean."

Robert smiled then quickly removed the smile from his face. "That may be a place to start, Detective. There have been rumours for years that original Manichaean scrolls had been buried in caves in the desert."

"Which desert?"

"The Taklamakan. Like everyone else persecuted in the West, the Manichaeans came across the Silk Road seeking sanctuary. The Church followed them. To evade Rome the Manichaeans were said to have buried their sacred texts then disappeared into the Middle Kingdom."

"China is the ocean that salts all rivers," Fong quoted quietly.

"What?"

"An old saying, Mr. Cowens. So the Manichaeans headed east for safety just as did your parents – and sister."

Robert looked at Fong trying to see if there was any sarcasm in the comment. There wasn't. "Yes. Like my parents and my sister." He rubbed his chin again and a smile slowly crossed his face. "I could let it be known to my associates that I have in my possession one of those original Manichaean scrolls and want to sell it. If this arsonist is a true believer it may be enough to draw him out."

"It may."

Robert nodded. "We have a deal then, Detective Zhong?"

"Write down all the information you have about your parents' time in Shanghai and whatever else you need to know. I will set my people to it."

"How long will it take?"

"It could take a while. I'll contact you when I know something, hopefully by exactly two months from today."

"Why then?"

"Why not? It's a friend's birthday."

Robert looked at him. Fong returned his stare. Finally Fong

said, "How long should it take to get in contact with our Manichaean friend?"

"Hard to tell. But if we're lucky it could be fast – very fast."

Fong turned toward the broken window and muttered, "It better be." Then he turned back to Robert. "What do you need to start this?"

"Let me out of here – that's a start."

Fong considered putting an electronic tracking cuff on Robert. But Fong had worn one himself for some time and wouldn't impose that misery on anyone else. "Give me your passport."

Robert handed it over.

"Do you have a cell phone, Mr. Cowens?"

Robert produced it from his jacket pocket. Fong jotted down the ten-digit local number then handed it back. As Robert reached for it Fong held his side of the phone so the two of them felt each other's pressure through the electronic device. "Don't switch it off. And carry it at all times. I'll be calling in every two hours. You don't answer me and I'll have you arrested and tossed into Ti Lan Chou Prison. You know what that is?"

"The political prison."

"Right," Fong said and released his end of the phone.

Robert pocketed the thing. Fong gave Robert his cell number. "Call me if anything and I mean anything begins to happen." Robert nodded then turned to go.

"Mr. Cowens."

Robert turned back to face Fong. The small man with the delicate features had his hand out. Robert took a step toward him and took the proffered hand. The two men, so very different, from such different worlds, felt the meeting as their palms touched. Neither would acknowledge it, but this was clearly the meeting of two very lonely men.

Angel Michael used the ID he'd stolen the first time he entered the Hua Shan Hospital to pass by security. It was late and the cleaning crews were reporting for work. He slid on his smock and grabbed a cleaner's cart. He wheeled past the reception desk and its two guards. They glanced at him then signalled for him to stop. They came over quickly and flipped open the covered area on the floor of the trolley. A stinky wash bucket with dirty bandages greeted their inquiring looks.

"Yow!" one of them said as he threw down the sheet that covered the area. "What a smell."

"Yeah, but instructions said for all the trolleys to be checked."

"Can I go, now?" Angel Michael asked.

"Lots of cleaning left to do?"

"Lots," Angel Michael said as he steered his cart toward the abortion ORs. "So they figured out the trick with the cart," he thought, "fine I planned for that – that's what windows are for, after all." He moved past several ORs and came to the sixth. Only the first and the sixth had windows. He went in and closed the door carefully behind him. Then he wheeled the trolley over to the window. Standing on top of the cart, he nimbly hauled himself up to the window ledge. He slipped on his rock-climbing shoes and with the rosin pouch at his side he started up the outside wall toward the roof. The crumbling masonry gave out beneath his feet twice but his hand strength was considerable; each time he dangled briefly then pulled himself up to another foothold.

On the roof he unearthed the cage with its gruesome contents from a pile of discarded shingle tiles and hooked it on his back. Going down was more complicated but no problem for a world-class rock climber like Angel Michael.

He put the cage down on the ground to the side of the window ledge and slid back into the surgery, standing on the cart. Then he heard the door open. He jumped down, grabbed a rag, and started cleaning the stainless steel surgical table. Four soldiers ran in with arms drawn. Angel Michael stood back and held up his hands. One of the soldiers barked out, "Turn around and put your hands up against the wall."

As Angel Michael turned he realized that the small window high up the wall was open! But the soldiers were so busy searching him that they never looked up. When they were done they shooed him out of the room with the instruction, "Go clean somewhere else."

Fong paced back and forth in the rear of the old theatre. Onstage technicians hung, dropped, then re-hung lights. Chinese theatre technicians were not theatre specialists. They were workmen – in this case, electricians – seconded to work on productions in the final days before opening. It was hardly an ideal situation.

Fong had already given the stage manager a note to deliver to Tuan Li. He was anxious to apologize. Insulting Tuan Li had been like insulting his dead wife, Fu Tsong. But just as he took a seat a female voice called his name. He turned. It was not Tuan Li. It was Lily.

And she was furious.

Angel Michael moved away from the surgeries and dragged his cart up the stairs. He didn't know this part of the hospital but he needed to find a way out to the courtyard to retrieve the cage and RDX explosive he'd left there. He tried the first two offices but they were locked. He reached for the knob on the third door, to the office right above the first OR, and the handle turned. He shut the door behind him and turned on the light. To his surprise this was not a single office but a warren of small labs. With a shock he realized that these were police forensic labs.

Then he saw the photo on the main desk. He'd seen the woman before – and the man – outside the hospital – speaking

English. She had been the one who had the antique fresco sent to the hospital that had interrupted his first attempt to plant his bomb at the Hua Shan Hospital. She was the one who upset his schedule so that the American newspapers were now claiming that there had been no second blast – that it was an industrial accident. This woman had cast doubt on his entire enterprise.

He picked up the photo. The two adults were huddled around a small creature – a baby. He pocketed the photo then hunted for an address. It didn't take him long to find it. To his delight it was a simple walk away – to the Shanghai Theatre Academy. Mani had said "a believer must fight those who would keep the light from the world."

And as Angel Michael made his way to the theatre academy that was precisely what he was planning to do.

Fong's cell phone rang as he and Lily entered their apartment. Lily looked at him – well not really looked, no, dared would be a more accurate description. She dared him to answer his cell phone. So he didn't. It continued to ring. Xiao Ming began to cry.

"Xiao Ming's crying," Fong said.

"I'm not deaf, Fong," snapped Lily and folded her arms across her chest. Fong's cell phone stopped ringing. There was a moment where the only sound in the room was Xiao Ming's sobbing. Fong looked at the fresco on the wall beside the window. The Western man seemed to radiate light and serenity. "We could use a bit of both of those in here, now," he thought. He reached over and turned on the overhead light.

"Turn that off."

He did.

"What are you smiling at, Fong. There's nothing funny here."

Xiao Ming's crying became more emphatic. Fong's cell phone rang again. "Lily, can this wait?"

"For what?"

"A better time. A time when . . ."

"When you can think of a good explanation for your behaviour? No. I don't think this can wait. And turn off that cell phone."

He did – mid-ring. Xiao Ming stopped crying instantly. The silence in the apartment was thick with possibilities. Lily bit her lip and turned away from Fong. Finally he said, "I don't deserve you."

"No. You don't."

A long silence.

"Well, at least we agree on that."

"This is not funny, Fong. Not funny. We are married. You are married to me. We have a baby. Fu Tsong is dead. I never asked you how or why she died. But she is dead. She must not come between us now." Suddenly she was crying. Through her tears she barked out, "I can't compete with a famous actress. Especially a famous dead actress." Then she stomped her foot and screamed, "Not fair. This is not fair."

Instantly, Xiao Ming began to wail. Fong's cell phone didn't ring because its ringer was turned off but he felt it vibrate in his pocket.

"Lily, listen to me. Lily."

"I'm listening."

"I do things. They sometimes hurt people. I don't mean to hurt people but sometimes I do."

"What things do you do that hurt people? Why do you hurt people? Why do you hurt me? Why were you in that theatre just now? What is happening between us?"

He took a deep breath. He felt as if he were in the middle of a swinging bridge over a vast gorge. He and Lily were some-how there together and he had set alight the rope cables on either end. The bridge was swinging and he had no idea who, if anyone, would make it back alive.

"I'm afraid."

"Of what?"

He took another deep breath. "I have always been alone Lily. With people, but alone. Fu Tsong helped me with that but only a little."

"And me? Do I help you with that? I'd prefer that you don't say her name in our home again, Fong."

That stunned him. "She was part of me."

"But not part of me or of us, Fong. You and me and Xiao Ming. Not part of us." She leaned against the wall.

"Okay."

"So answer the question."

Fong sensed that the rope cable on their swinging bridge was beginning to fray, "Do you help? That question?"

"That question, Fong."

The bridge began to rock violently, "No, I'm sorry but you don't help with that, Lily."

It was as if the cable snapped. Lily gave way and slid down the wall she was leaning against so that she was on the floor with her knees up by her shoulders. She began to cry. Xiao Ming joined in.

Another cable snapped. Fong plummeted toward the roiling water of the gorge beneath.

Fong went into their bedroom and picked up Xiao Ming. When he came back into the living room, Lily was on her feet drying her tears. Without saying a word she took Xiao Ming from his arms and headed toward the door.

As she reached for the door handle Fong knew he should ask, "Where are you going?" but he didn't. When she threw open the door both of them were surprised to see Captain Chen.

"Sorry. Am I interrupting something, Miss Lily?"

"Lily, not Miss Lily and no you are not, Captain Chen. Xiao Ming and I were just on our way to my mother's place. We thought we'd spend some time there. Perhaps a decade or two." She pushed past Captain Chen who looked in at Fong. "Sorry, sir, but you didn't answer your cell phone."

Fong looked at the young man. "Have you found something?"

"About the cage, yes. I think I found who made them."

As Fong and Chen raced out they passed right by a beautiful young Chinese man – a man whose photograph they had drawn from a VHS tape – Angel Michael. The man watched Fong and Captain Chen go and then turned in the other direction and followed Lily and Xiao Ming. Mani was clearly guiding him now. Mani had divided the family for him. A plan was coming into clear focus. The pathway to return the light was opening before him.

The ancient man sat waiting for Fong to speak. If, as Chen suspected, he had learned his metallurgy during the Great Leap Forward the man could well be in his eighties. Fong noted the man's fingers. Long. Tapered. Supple. "What was it with artists and beautiful hands?" Fong wondered.

Fong sat opposite the man. He identified himself and began to explain why he was there.

The man stopped him. "Your companion, Captain Chen, has already explained the circumstances of your visit."

There was a sharpness in the man's voice and a confidence – as if he'd been interrogated many times before.

Fong thought he knew why. "Did you have a hard time of it during the Cultural Revolution?"

"I am an artist. The Red Guards hated artists."

Simple. Straightforward. Clearly true.

"But why?" Fong found himself asking.

"We can see the beauty. They cannot."

Again simple. Again true.

"Do you know the use your cages have been put to?"

The man nodded, his face neutral.

"Who bought the cages?"

"A man."

"Which man?"

"He was very careful when we met. He contacted me and had me meet him at a restaurant in the Pudong."

"Which one?"

"I don't know its name but it was set up like an American restaurant, a diner, I believe they are called. I was instructed to sit in the farthest booth from the door and face the back of the restaurant. He sat in the booth just forward of me and ordered me not to look back at him. My eyes are not very good. I'm old. I don't see well at night and the lights in that place were turned down very low. He explained what he wanted and handed me plans."

"How many times did you meet him?"

"Just that once."

"How did he pick up the cages?"

"I left them for him in a locker at the North Train Station. He'd given me the key."

"Was he old, young?" Fong reined in his growing frustration and continued, "Please think, we need your help."

The old man digested that and pulled himself up to his full height. He spoke softly. "It was hard for me to tell."

Chen spread out the three photos on the table. "One of these men, perhaps, Grandpa?"

The old artist looked at the three photographs. He put aside the two middle-aged men and stared at the young man with the briefcase. Then he opened a desk drawer and drew out a magnifying glass. He put it close to the photograph. Fong saw that he was looking at the man's hands. Of course, the man had handed over the plans. The old man would have seen the hands!

The old artist began to nod and held the pictures.

Fong stared at the photograph. The image there was so young. So clear. So free of doubt. So . . . luminous. Without looking at the old artist Fong said, "Him."

The old artist nodded.

"Do you think he saw the beauty, sir?" Chen asked the cage maker.

The old man thought about that for a moment then said, "No. But I believe he saw something else."

"What?" asked Fong.

"Something . . ." his voice faltered. Then he tried again, "Something, somehow, entirely different, foreign."

Fong thought about that for a moment but could make no sense of it. He took the photo and strode toward the door. With his hand on the doorknob he stopped and turned back to the older man. "Why did you do it?"

"Do what?"

"Make the cages for him. Surely you knew there was something odd about his request."

"Something odd?" the old man murmured as a small smile creased his face. "Yes, Detective, I guess there was something odd in his request. There was also two thousand American dollars. Enough to buy me all the materials I will need till my passing." Then he abruptly spat on the ground and his voice turned hard, "I did nothing illegal. What I made harmed no one. This is not the Cultural Revolution. You are not Red Guards. Now go away."

"How many cages did you make for him?" Chen asked.

"Four," the man replied.

"Has he picked them all up?" Chen asked.

"Days ago."

Fong strode back to the table. "This man covers his tracks. He killed the nurse who helped him. He'll kill you too."

"Only if he finds me, Detective."

"We found you."

"No. Your ugly friend found me. How did you manage that, Captain Chen?"

"People tell me things they often will not tell others."

"Ah," the man smiled. "An advantage of a modest appearance." Then he quoted, "We are all granted a boon, although sometimes that specialness is hard, at first, to see."

CHAPTER NINETEEN

AND THE ROOK TAKES THE QUEEN

Angel Michael waited outside the apartment block – one of the old Soviet-styled horrors. He didn't follow Lily and the baby into the place for fear that the building warden would note his presence. Instead, he stood on the sidewalk and mixed with a crowd of Shanghanese commenting on a game of Go being played by two elderly gentlemen in Mao jackets. The crowd clearly favoured the man using the black stones, but Angel Michael quickly saw that the elderly man using the white stones was a much better player. Every feint white made, attracted black's eye. Whole sections of the board began to close off to black without him even knowing it as he concentrated on one of the many diversions black set up.

Angel Michael understood the value of a diversion. He was planning one of his own at that very moment. The level of security at the Hua Shan Hospital was very high. He'd gotten the cage and the RDX to the courtyard outside the window of the operating room but he needed time in the surgery itself to set the detonator. He needed a distraction – and a cover – and he thought he knew the key to both: Xiao Ming.

Lily came out of the building and headed in the direction of the Hua Shan Hospital. Shortly thereafter, Lily's mother came out of the building wheeling her granddaughter as if she were a tiny queen. Matthew remembered the chess games with the man he called his father. He remembered how even a queen can be a diversion. He remembered that bad chess players watched the queen. Good ones knew that although the queen had mobility and power, she was not the point of the game. The almost immobile king was. The baby Xiao Ming was only the queen. The Hua Shan Hospital abortion surgery was the king. Direct their eyes toward the queen long enough and their king would be vulnerable.

Matthew followed the queen and her grand dame down the road. He kept his distance and they led him to their oh-so-logical end. The queen, of course, goes to the palace – the Shanghai Children's Palace. Matthew paid his admission, avoided the drama club kids, and followed the queen. Xiao Ming and her grandmother were met at a side door that opened to a surprisingly Western-style plastic playground. The place was a daycare of some sort. By the way the two were greeted they were clearly regulars. Lily's mom took her leave of Xiao Ming with a big kiss. The child smiled.

Once Lily's mother was gone, Matthew took a small digital camera from his pocket, zoomed in, and took a shot of Xiao Ming. Then another. Then a third.

A daycare worker came up to him. "She's a lovely girl."

"Yeah, we're crazy about her."

"We haven't seen . . ."

"No. I'm usually at work by now. I'm with Special Investigations."

"A police officer?"

He smiled and took one last photo of his queenly diversion then asked when Xiao Ming's grandmother usually returned to pick up the child.

"Usually around three." Then confidentially the woman added, "I think she plays Mah Jong, I hope you won't arrest her." She laughed.

Angel Michael joined in her laughter then told the woman that he'd be back to pick up Xiao Ming today. "We'll give the old lady a break. Give her time to win back her losses." She laughed at that too. He went to leave. The woman called after him, "Don't you want to take a picture of me?"

He paused then smiled. He pressed the flash button but not the "capture" button. The woman smiled. Matthew didn't.

As he left the Children's Palace, Matthew pocketed the digital camera and put on a pair of sunglasses. It was going to be a hot day and it would get hotter – much hotter, Angel Michael thought. He took in the landmarks. Fine. Not far from the Hua Shan Hospital or the Shanghai Theatre Academy. Almost halfway between the fighting parents. Good.

He began to think about the courtyard of the Hua Shan Hospital – and the things he'd stowed there.

Copies of Angel Michael's picture were being rushed around the city. Every hotel, every restaurant, every flophouse was scoured. Just before two o'clock in the afternoon a weary cop approached the front desk of the Shanghai Metron Hotel. Angel Michael spotted him the moment he entered the lobby. Cops walk as if they are important – weary, hard-working, but righteously important. When the man drew out the photo, Angel Michael guessed that they had found the cage maker. He knew he should have ended that one's earthly woes. But it didn't matter now. He checked his watch. Four hours and twelve minutes and the sixth operating theatre at the Hua Shan Hospital would deliver his final message – which he still needed to move into place.

In fact, the presence of the cop played right into his hands. He ducked out of the lobby and ran up to the second floor. From there he took an elevator to his room. He grabbed the few things that he needed then flipped open his computer screen and downloaded his favourite digital picture of Xiao Ming. He hit F2 and the pre-designed program began to roll. Matthew left the room with a backpack over his shoulder and headed down the service elevator. Even as he made his way out the back entrance of the building, the hotel manager was opening his room and letting in the cop.

Forty minutes later, Fong stood in Angel Michael's room but his eyes were not searching the place for clues. They were glued to the computer screen where an image of Xiao Ming trapped in a cage was turning round and round and round while a message scrolled across the bottom: *"I am in the light – and your daughter is with me there."*

CHAPTER TWENTY

BAITING AN ANGEL'S TRAP

obert Cowens stood up as his translator entered the restaurant. He had picked her favourite place, a small Japanese restaurant discreetly tucked away on a side street in the embassy district. The place was so clean that Robert always felt underwashed when he went there. Well, he'd also felt that way the few times he'd been in Japan. Their accent on hygiene was really a little much. This "accent" was even more evident when one had just stepped out of the harsh realities of Shanghai street life. His translator took off her round glasses and sat quietly with her hands folded on her lap. He offered her the dish of pickled pumpkin seeds. She declined. He ordered an appetizer and green tea. She didn't speak.

Finally he asked, "How was your interview?"

"Interview, Mr. Cowens?"

"With Detective Zhong?"

"I didn't . . ."

"Please. We've worked together for a long time, you and I. I have never thought of you in any way as stupid. Please don't think that I am."

She blushed – an unusual colour on the flawless Asian skin of her rounded cheeks.

"Fine, now I want you to get in touch with your contacts."

Her eyes widened. "Contacts, Mr. Cowens?"

"Again, I ask you not to treat me as if I am stupid. I've known from the beginning that you have contacts. That everything you and I talk about 'moves' to other places. So I want you to convince your contacts that I have in my possession an original Manichaean scroll all the way from the Taklamakan Desert. You can do that, can't you?"

The green tea arrived. She reached for the pot but he beat her to it and poured for her. As she brought the steaming liquid to her lips he said, "This is important to me. Understood?"

She nodded and said, "*Dui.*"

It was only at that point that Devil Robert realized he had conducted the entire conversation in Mandarin. He smiled.

She looked at him questioningly.

"How's my Mandarin?" he asked in Mandarin.

"Getting better, Mr. Cowens. Getting much better." She put her green tea down and stood.

"Won't you stay to eat?"

"No, Mr. Cowens. If this is important to you, I need to start right away. I should have a response for you soon."

He nodded and poured tea for himself as she left the restaurant.

Fong knew he was shouting into his cell phone but he couldn't stop himself. When Lily finally got on the line she shouted right back at him, "How dare you order my forensic people around, who the hell do you . . .?"

"Where's Xiao Ming!"

"With my mother as she . . ."

"Are you sure?"

"Yes, every morning my mother . . ."

"Can you contact her, Lily?"

Suddenly there was fear in her voice as she said slowly, "Why?"

Fong paused. He heard Lily gasp. "Where does your mother usually take Xiao Ming, Lily?"

"I don't know . . ."

"Think!"

And Lily did. She began to reel off places and Fong relayed them to his officers. Within an hour more than 40 percent of the officers assigned to guard the Hua Shan Hospital were out on the streets looking for Fong and Lily's baby.

Angel Michael arrived to pick up Xiao Ming. He carried a digitally doctored photo of the baby and the grandmother with him standing beside them, just in case he was challenged. But there was no need. The woman in charge of the daycare at the Children's Palace was happy to see the handsome young man again. It crossed Angel Michael's mind that what would really have pleased this woman was being touched the way his French teacher had made him touch her. Angel Michael breathed away the nausea that came with that thought and allowed a smile to his beautifully shaped lips. The lady smiled back at him and bobbed a bow.

As Angel Michael left the Children's Palace, Xiao Ming began to struggle in his arms. She did not cry out. No. But she looked deep into his eyes. It almost spooked him.

Twenty minutes later, Fong ran into the Children's Palace. Five minutes after that, Angel Michael entered the largest abortion facility in all of China – the Hua Shan Hospital. Xiao Ming was in his arms. He carried a shopping bag. No one stopped him or even asked him to present ID. What kind of bomber carried a baby?

With Xiao Ming in the crook of his arm he waited for a moment until the front reception desk was at its busiest then put the note on the counter and slipped back into the crowd. Ten minutes later, one of the three harried receptionists opened the envelope and shouted for a security guard.

Less than ninety seconds after that, Fong's phone rang and he went pale.

"What?" demanded Lily.

"Another note at the Hua Shan Hospital." He called his head of security. "Evacuate the hospital! Contact Wu Fan-zi!"

He looked back to Lily. She was ashen. "The man who wrote the note has Xiao Ming, doesn't he?"

Fong nodded.

Suddenly Lily was screaming at him. "She's your daughter, Fong. Do something. Do something!"

Angel Michael took advantage of the chaos of the Hua Shan Hospital's third evacuation in four days to slip past the few remaining guards. Five minutes later, he entered the hospital's sixth abortion surgery. He put Xiao Ming on the table, climbed up to the window, and grabbed the titanium cage with its grisly contents and the RDX explosive he'd stashed in the courtyard just outside. Back in the operating room he took out the complicated timing device he'd carried in the shopping bag and wired it to the explosive. Then he placed the titanium cage beneath the table and stood back to admire his handiwork. On the operating table, Xiao Ming lay very still, watching him. For a moment he paused, then he grabbed the girl and headed out into the gathering chaos. He dropped the remaining contents of the shopping bag as he did – decoy bombs.

As he rushed down the front steps of the hospital his cell phone rang. It wasn't a familiar number. He punched his directory ID and it came up with a name that Angel Michael only vaguely recognized. It was a trader he had contacted six months ago, when he was first setting up operations in Shanghai. At that time he had been trolling for basic tradable objects but his list included an interest in any Manichaean writings.

He looked at the number again then at Xiao Ming.

"So, little one," he said in Mandarin, "should I return this call or not?"

Xiao Ming looked at him closely. She noted the movement of his lips then did as she always did – she imitated what she saw. The man smiled at the baby, "Good time, bad time, opportunity only knocks once." He punched the talk button.

Fong's cell rang. "What?"

"It's Robert Cowens. I believe I've made contact."

"It's too late."

"For what?"

"Never mind."

"What do you want me to do, Detective?"

Fong had no idea. Too many things were in motion. "Don't do anything. No. Try to set up a meeting then get back to me."

Fong hung up but his phone immediately rang again. "Zhong Fong."

"We're going in, Fong," said Wu Fan-zi's confident voice.

"Good."

Wu Fan-zi hung up. Moments later it occurred to Fong that Wu Fan-zi had said "we." Who the hell was the "we" part of "we"?

Angel Michael knew that without another diversion they may well have time to disarm the bomb despite its complex timing device and the decoys. He needed to cause a significant fuss to draw fire his way – looking at Xiao Ming he corrected himself, "our way." Then it occurred to him. How simple. In a single-child society, children are the most valuable of all commodities. And where were there many, many children in one place? The Children's Palace . . . of course.

* * *

As Fong raced toward the Hua Shan Hospital his cell phone rang. It was the head of security at the Children's Palace. A man was holding sixty-five children and their teacher hostage on the second floor of the building!

CHAPTER TWENTY-ONE

BOMBS

The cell phone broke up so badly that Wu Fan-zi couldn't be sure he understood what Fong was saying – then it went dead. Anything could have interfered with the connection but Wu Fan-zi wondered if somehow it was his own anxiety that was causing it. He looked to Joan Shui at his side. He saw her caught within the thickness of his glass face shield. "Who else in the world can look good in bomb protective gear?" he wondered. Then another thought flitted, unwelcome, through his mind, "Am I going to lose her so soon?"

The phone crackled, then spat into life. "Status, Wu Fan-zi?" Fong was shouting.

"Fong, you're cutting out on me."

"We've got a situation here."

"Where are you?"

"Back at the Children's Palace on Nanjing Lu. He's holding a whole room of children with him and – my daughter as well."

"Who is?"

"The bomber."

"Fong . . ."

"He claims that if we disarm the bomb he'll start killing the children. He's already killed their teacher."

"But how could he know what's . . ."

"I don't know. Tell me what you have there, Wu Fan-zi." Fong's voice was tight.

Wu Fan-zi took a deep breath and then said, "A complex device with an obvious timer. I've never seen a system set up like this. We already disarmed two dummies on our way in but now that we are in the abortion surgery I'm not sure how to proceed."

"Wu Fan-zi, the *New York Times* contacted my office. They received an e-mail stating that there will be an explosion at precisely 4 p.m. at the Hua Shan Hospital. It had a digital photo of a fetus in a cage and another lunatic phrase about the light finally coming. Is it possible that he could have set the bomb for 4 p.m.?"

"Of course, it's possible, Fong," Wu Fan-zi shouted back.

"That would give you less than fifteen minutes," Fong stated.

"Maybe he's lying."

"Maybe he's not." Fong waited for a moment, then continued, "Are you alone there?"

"No. Joan Shui's with me."

"Get her out of there, Wu Fan-zi." Silence greeted Fong's request so he said it a second time. Still silence. Finally Fong said, "Do you need her help in disarming the bomb?"

Wu Fan-zi looked at Joan Shui then said into the phone, "No."

"Do you care about her?"

Joan Shui reached for the phone but Wu Fan-zi held it to one side. Then he put his hand on her arm and said into the phone, "Yes."

"Then get her out of there, Wu Fan-zi."

"Do me a favour, Fong?"

"Sure. Name it."

"If I don't . . ."

"You will."

"I don't think so this time. I want you to celebrate my fifty-third birthday – even if I'm not there."

After a brief silence, Fong said, "Sure."

"It's exactly two months from today."

"I know that. We'll drink the night away – you and me and Joan Shui."

Fong couldn't be sure but he thought he heard Wu Fan-zi stifle a laugh – or could it be a cry. Fong couldn't picture that. But the phone line between the two men had somehow gotten far too intimate. Too close. Fong shook the image of a terrified Wu Fan-zi away, then said quickly, "See you at the party if not before."

Wu Fan-zi didn't reply. He simply disconnected the line and turned to Joan Shui. "Is everyone out safely?"

"Yes."

After a long pause he said, "No. You're not out."

"I won't leave you here alone," she said.

"You will."

"I . . ."

"You have no choice. I'm ordering you to go."

She nodded slowly and touched his face mask. She was shocked to see tears rolling down his cheeks.

"Go." Then softly he added, "Please."

"But I just met you."

"All the more reason to leave." He looked at the device sitting beneath the surgical table. It had six coloured wires coming from it. No device needs more than three. He looked at her and raised his shoulders questioningly. "Any guesses?"

"You want me to guess which wire to cut?"

"Unless you know which one I should cut."

"I don't."

"Neither do I." He took off his face mask. So did she. "So, guess."

"Green. Cut the green. I've always hated the colour green."

She touched his lips softly then moved out of the room.

"Joan?"

She stopped and looked back at him.

"It's my fifty-third birthday two months from now."

"Going to have a party?"

"Fong's throwing one for me."

"I'll be there," she said.

"Good. It's a date. Now go."

He glanced at his watch. It was eleven minutes before four o'clock. He gave Joan a full ten minutes to get safely out of the Hua Shan Hospital then flipped his face shield into place and reached for his wire cutters.

*   *   *

Robert Cowens called Fong. "Where are you, Detective?"

"Not anywhere that you can help me."

"I think I . . . might be able to help . . ."

"You can't help here!" Fong punched the off button of his cell phone.

But not before Robert heard, quiet, as if deep in the background, the dharma kids' unforgettable rendition of "Ok-ra-homa."

The explosion at the Hua Shan Hospital tore a huge hole in the side of the building. The air that rushed in fed a massive fireball that raced along an upper corridor and blasted out all the windows. It rained glass and bricks and what little remained of the earthly existence of Wu Fan-zi on the crowd below. Joan stood very still and reached a hand to her belly. She began to cry – like she hadn't cried since she had been a child.

Fong opened the door to the large room and stepped in leaving the distant sounds of dharma kids' song behind him. He had chosen not to evacuate the children from the rest of the building and insisted on going in to confront the bomber alone. He left Chen to keep Lily and the other cops outside.

The room in which the bomber held the children had originally been a ballroom. Up above was a balustrade that encircled the entire space from which guests could watch the dancers. Now the room was a big open space with a raised circular dais in the centre. In the middle of the platform the beautiful man from the photograph stood holding Xiao Ming in the crook of his left arm. In his right hand he held one of the Tibetan's razor-sharp swolta blades. The other sixty or so children were sitting, back to the man, with their feet dangling over the sides of the platform. All faced out. Some cried. Many had urinated in their pants. All showed the extremis of fear on their faces. The teacher who Angel Michael had executed ten minutes ago, to prove he was serious, lay on the floor – the fresh swolta cut across her throat still leaking crimson.

"Message conveyed?" the man shouted toward Fong.

Fong nodded.

"Good. So now we wait – we wait for the light to come."

There was a silence and then a voice came from above, "Don't you need this to make the light come?"

The man looked up to the balustrade. Devil Robert stood there holding the fake scroll he had received from the Chinese men on the Bund Promenade his first day back in Shanghai. Robert undid the ribbon and, holding one end, with a mighty heave tossed the other end toward the ceiling. The scroll unwound in an elongated flutter and seemed to hang in the air.

Angel Michael looked up.

Fong reached inside his coat and felt the butt of Chen's pistol. Suddenly Xiao Ming began to cry. Her howls immediately set off the other children.

Robert heard the crying and for a moment felt the sick

sensation of being seven years old and hearing his brother: "*No, Mommy. No Mommy no.*" He swallowed hard then pulled out a Zippo lighter and scraped it along his pant leg. The flame leapt up almost six inches high. Robert used all his will power to control his fear and whipped his end of the scroll hard so the rest of the thing rose like a dragon's tail.

A quiet took the room.

Robert looked at Fong. He saw Fong's hand pull out the gun.

Robert's voice bloomed inside Fong's head: "I thought you were a lousy shot."

Fong answered inside Robert's head: "I am."

Devil Robert shouted at Angel Michael, "It's real. No Islam Akhun forgery here."

Angel Michael gasped and reached upward, toward the scroll.

Holding the Zippo aloft Robert shouted, "Let them go or I light this."

Angel Michael screamed, "No."

Robert touched the flame to the treated parchment. The paper whooshed into life, the flame leaping along its length aided by the chemical treatment used to make the scroll appear to be ancient. The paper raced fire across the space like a flash of heat lightning on a moonless night.

All eyes in the room looked up.

Then the part of the scroll that Robert held in his hand burst into flame. The smell of his own burning flesh brought a rush of memory to Robert: *No, Mommy. No Mommy no.* But now Robert wasn't sure if it was his brother's voice or his own.

Angel Michael opened his arms to the burning pathway above him, a luminous smile suddenly appearing on his face. For an instant Robert saw the innocent child Angel Michael had been, not the madman he now was.

Angel Michael put Xiao Ming on the dais then lay down

beside her. He turned the baby's head so she faced away from him. Then he slipped his even-sided cross from his neck and placed it in his mouth.

Fong raced toward the dais, the gun at his side.

Angel Michael raised the swolta knife and moved it toward Xiao Ming's throat – an arm's-length away.

A potent thought bloomed in Fong's mind: "It was a sacrifice – the baby in the construction pit was not made to watch the father die – the baby was sacrificed by the father!"

The swolta touched Xiao Ming's throat.

Fong raised his gun. But as he pressed the trigger everything changed. Suddenly he was in a modern room with a curved staircase at the far side. Music was playing. People were dressed for a celebration of some sort. A hand tapped him on the shoulder and he turned. Commissioner Hu, the man in charge when Fong had first joined Special Investigations and who everyone referred to as His Huness, smiled his connected party smile and said to Fong, "Keep your eyes open, you're here on business."

The guy always knew how to ruin a good time.

"Right, sir," Fong said. He was surprised at how young his voice sounded. Then he recognized where this was – no, what this was. It was a party after a performance at the Shanghai Theatre Academy. He and a few of the other candidates for Special Investigations had been tapped to provide security because they were cops and could speak enough English to overhear conversations between the Chinese actors and the many visiting foreign dignitaries.

It was the night that he had first met Fu Tsong, his deceased wife.

The band was playing – something forties, swinging. He moved toward the music and struck up a conversation with one of the men listening. "How was the play?"

"Sensational. This new actress Fu Tsong is truly amazing."

"What was it?"

"*Twelfth Night*. She plays a girl who dresses as a boy, then reveals herself at the end as a woman."

"Sounds like a Peking Opera."

"In fact, at first I thought it was a Peking Opera then I read the notes in the program."

"It's not Peking Opera then?"

"Plot sounds like it but no. British. By a guy named Shakespeare. Hey look, there she is."

Fong looked. On the sweeping set of stairs stood an extraordinary, delicate creature flanked by two men. She seemed to glide effortlessly down the steps. At the bottom she nodded to the people waiting to talk to her. Then she headed toward the door. Halfway there the band completed their tune. She stopped to offer her applause.

When she did she saw Fong for the first time.

She tilted her head slightly and took a step toward him. He remembered little else except that they had danced together that night in a small bar. Then found a taxi and took it down to the river. They walked till a clear dawn came up over the Huangpo – the Huangpo that led to the mighty Yangtze, that in turn led to the sea. The details of the evening were lost to Fong. It was as if they had happened to someone else.

"It's ephemeral, Fong," said Fu Tsong. Then she laughed. "In fact, it could just as easily not have happened at all."

"Look."

Fong looked where she pointed. He found himself in the same room, with the same conversations both with his Huness and the man who had seen *Twelfth Night*. "No. British. By a guy named Shakespeare. Hey look, there she is."

And there she was again. Fu Tsong glided effortlessly down the sweeping steps. At the bottom she nodded to the people waiting to talk to her and then she headed toward the door just as she had done before. Halfway there the band completed their tune with the exact same ending as the other time. Fu Tsong stopped to offer her applause but this time the band picked up a tag and segued directly into a more modern number.

Fu Tsong threw back her head and laughed as she continued to the door and left – without, even for a moment, casting a glance in Fong's direction.

Fong looked down – his finger was pulling the trigger of the gun.

The shot thundered in his ears.

Just a glance – or a non-glance and a life changes. The slightest pressure on the metal of a pistol's trigger and a life ends.

A viciously bright flash – a young man – a beautiful young man – a Chinese man – whose associates called Angel Michael – lay dead on the floor – a single bullet hole in his forehead – an even-sided cross half in and half out of his mouth. There is remarkably little blood. The silence in the room is momentarily profound.

Then the children scream – and life continues.

Fong let the gun fall and turned away. It was a lucky shot. He knew it. He could as easily have killed Xiao Ming as Angel Michael.

Police officers rushed into the room from all sides. Crying children and shouting cops. At the height of the mayhem Fong saw Captain Chen leap up on the dais, grab Xiao Ming, and hold her tight to his chest. Lily was only a step behind him.

But Fong didn't move toward his wife and child.

He didn't know why or why his eyes were drawn upward to the black cinder of the scroll that rose on hidden currents and twisted and turned like a thing that although dead – refused to die.

AFTER

Fong wasn't surprised how out of place Robert Cowens seemed in the small canteen at the Shanghai Theatre Academy. No one in Shanghai has a kitchen so everyone eats in places like the canteen. The food was inexpensive and reasonably good but not really open to the public so it was only the rare foreigner who found their way into such places. Sometimes, because the canteen was connected to the theatre academy, Fong would see foreigners – usually guest directors – seated at the rickety tables picking carefully through the food in front of them. He recalled one such Caucasian who had dragged his translator to the canteen to identify the meat he had been eating for weeks. When the white man came to the table with a dish of the mystery meat, the translator's face went a little pale. "This," he'd said pointing at the plate of breaded, deep-fried meat covered in a sweet brown sauce. "This. What kind of meat is this?"

The man's translator had taken a breath then put on her best smile and said, "Chicken. It's chicken."

The man had looked at her and replied, "You won't understand this but I've had chicken every Friday night for my entire life and I've never seen a piece of chicken like this."

The translator had nodded then said, "Ah. But this is thin chicken."

The man looked at her with a strange expression on his face. "Thin chicken?"

The translator gave a small apologetic smile and raised her arm from the elbow then moved her hand back and forth to indicate the movements of the head of a snake. "Very thin chicken."

The man's face darkened and he croaked out the word, "Snake?"

She'd nodded and said, "It's very good for you. Especially now, in winter."

"So I've been eating snake all this time?"

She nodded.

He shrugged. "Fuck it – it tastes good – and I feel particularly . . ."

"Virile?" she asked. "Snake is a man's food."

The memory made Fong smile.

"What're you smiling about, you old thief?" said Robert Cowens as he sat down beside Fong.

Fong was not even a little surprised that Robert carried a plate of deep-fried cobra covered in a goopy brown sauce. "What are you wagging your head about, Detective Zhong?"

"Nothing."

"How's the food in this place?"

"Virile."

"What?"

"The chief smokes while he cooks, so check for butts."

Robert took a large mouthful of the cobra and sighed. "It's good."

"I'm glad," Fong said. "How's the hand?"

"The burn was deep so it only healed partially."

"Does it hurt still?"

"No. It just reminds me – of things."

Fong looked at the man across from him, "So to what do I owe the pleasure of your company this evening?" he asked in mock surprise.

He mocked back, "I was hungry. I was in Shanghai. I thought it would be nice to see you."

Fong smiled, then said, "For a lawyer, you are a very poor liar."

"I'll take that as a compliment."

"Do."

"It's two months. I held up my end of the bargain. Now you hold up yours."

Fong looked at the white man closely. Beneath the table he fingered the envelope that contained the details of a business transaction entered into in January 1944. "May I ask you a question?"

Robert sighed. "If you have to."

"I don't have to. I am asking your permission."

"Sure."

"Were you close to your father?"

"Close? You mean did I care about my father?"

"Please. I am trying to be helpful. I lost my father when I was six. I only have the vaguest memory of him. I have no way of knowing if sons grow close to their fathers as they get older."

"Okay. That's fair. Yes. I was close to my father. Very close."

Fong nodded then said, "If that is the case I don't think you want to know what my investigations have found."

Robert let that sink in. "The truth . . ."

". . . will set you free? I doubt that Mr. Cowens."

"Did you find my sister Rivkah?"

"Yes. She died of malaria in the 1947 outbreak."

Robert took that blow right to the face. He flushed then rocked back in his chair. He pushed his food away. "That bastard!"

"Which bastard, Mr. Cowens?"

"That son of a bitch Silas Darfun!!"

"Wrong son of a bitch, Mr. Cowens."

Devil Robert stopped in his tracks as if he were in a long tunnel and had just seen the light of a train coming straight toward him. He couldn't speak. He felt himself go very hot then suddenly cold. And in his heart he knew.

"Silas Darfun was a great man, Mr. Cowens. He saved many people. I may not have liked the way that he made his money but I am very much in favour of the way he spent what he had. Children of all races and colours were raised by him and his Chinese wife. Many are powerful people today because of what he offered them. Your sister was never in his care. If she had been she would have been returned at the end of the war like all the others that he harboured."

Then in a voice from far away Robert heard himself asking, "Then who had her?"

"Silas offered to look after your sister but would not pay money for her." Fong placed a document on the table. "Your sister was sold to a factory that used small children to climb into machinery and untwine the threads of the textiles when they clogged the gears."

"But my mother would never have . . ."

Fong looked at the man across from him and then Robert was crying. He knew. "It wasn't my mother, was it?"

Fong shook his head. "Your father was a diabetic?"

Robert nodded through his tears.

"It must have been hard to find insulin in Shanghai during the war."

Robert stood. In his mind he saw his mother – *No, Mommy. No Mommy no.* All those years of thinking it was his mad mother when in fact his father had been the one. Old Europeans and their secrets. Old Europeans and their fucking secrets.

Fong offered a napkin to Robert and he took it. To Robert's surprise somehow a load had been lifted from him. He brushed aside the tears and felt lighter. He nodded his head several times allowing the new family history to jog into place. Then he sat.

"Thank you."

"I'm sorry it came out as it did."

"Me too – no, not true. I'm not sorry. Sad yes, but not sorry." Fong nodded.

Robert looked around. "Where's your wife?"

Fong instinctively retreated to his privacy then thought about it a moment and returned. "With Captain Chen. You met him . . ."

"The bovine young man?"

"Bovine means cowlike?"

"Yes."

"Yes with the bovine young man."

Robert looked at Fong hard – "With, as in lives with?"

"Yes," said Fong. "They share many things. They are a better couple than she and I."

"And the baby?"

"She stays with me when I can manage. I have . . ." Fong didn't complete his thought because over Robert's shoulder he saw Joan Shui walk into the restaurant and raise her hand to him. Robert sensed her approach and turned.

He looked back at Fong questioningly.

Fong raised his shoulders and said, "A little faith and things work out, Mr. Cowens."

Robert pulled out a chair for Joan Shui who offered her hand to him. He took it and was amazed by the supple pleasure of her touch.

She took off her coat. She was wearing a large T-shirt that had emblazoned on its front: LIFE IS A JOURNEY, NOT SOME STUPID GUIDED TOUR.

As she moved toward the kitchen both men watched her. Then Robert turned to Fong and said, "I'm happy for you."

"Thank you. May I offer you a piece of advice?"

After a moment Robert said, "Certainly."

"You think you are back in Shanghai just to find out about your sister but that is not the only reason you are here. You just won't admit it. Please don't try to protest. You will have to have a little faith and call her."

Robert sat very still. "I assume you have Tuan Li's phone number."

"I'm a cop so of course I do."

"Good." Fong flipped him his cell phone and said, "Have a little faith, make the call."

As Robert dialled, Joan Shui returned from the kitchen bearing a large chocolate cake with a single brilliant candle lit in the middle. Every eye in the canteen watched as she moved toward the table and deposited the cake in its centre. "It's Wu Fan-zi's fifty-third birthday," she said.

Fong smiled sadly.

Joan met his smile.

Together they blew out the candle and – as an act of faith – made a wish.

*   *   *

"I'm porous with travel fever
But so happy to be on my own"

"Hejira" by Joni Mitchell